Fire Year

Fire Year

stories

Jason K. Friedman

WINNER OF THE 2012

MARY MCCARTHY PRIZE IN SHORT FICTION

SELECTED BY SALVATORE SCIBONA

Sarabande  Books

LOUISVILLE, KENTUCKY

Managing Editor
Sarabande Books, Inc.
2234 Dundee Road, Suite 200
Louisville, KY 40205

Library of Congress Cataloging-in-Publication Data

Friedman, Jason.
[Short stories. Selections]
Fire year : stories / Jason K. Friedman. — First edition.
    pages cm. — (The Mary McCarthy Prize in Short Fiction)
"Winner of the 2012 Mary McCarthy Prize in Short Fiction,
Selected by Salvatore Scibona"—T.p. verso.
ISBN 978-1-936747-64-1 (paperback : acid-free paper)
I. Title.
PS3606.R564F57 2013
813'.6—dc23

2013005928

Cover art: *Beacon #4 (482)* by David King. Provided courtesy of the
artist (davidkingcollage.com).
Cover and text design by Kirkby Gann Tittle.
Manufactured in Canada.
This book is printed on acid-free paper.
Sarabande Books is a nonprofit literary organization.

"Blue" appeared in *Moment* magazine, November/December 2011.

The Kentucky Arts Council, the state arts agency,
supports Sarabande Books with state tax dollars and
federal funding from the National Endowment for the
Arts.

For Jeffrey

First reader, partner in everything

CONTENTS

Foreword

"[I]n my country," says the homesick priest in *A Farewell to Arms,* "it is understood that a man may love God. It is not a dirty joke."

In one way or another, the question whether love—both the love of God and secular love—must always decay into a joke animates each of the stories in the terrific collection you hold in your hands. *Fire Year* is about the vulnerability of love to sneers, snorts, junior-high-cafeteria abuse, disproof, disdain, and even to our own later laments that our fondest imaginings have misled us.

In the opening story, Aaron, "a puny and contemptible figure" at the narrator's bar mitzvah party, warns him of the social consequences of reading from the Torah with such overt devotion:

> "You were swaying."
> "You're supposed to do that."
> "Yeah, but you looked like you meant it."

In fact the narrator *does* mean it. "In those days," he will recall, "it was religion alone that lifted me out of despair." In the domain of current literary fashion, a narrator who cops to *despair* (forget about the hope of escaping it through anything so unironic as orthodox religion) is inviting zingers from the wisenheimer brigade. But among the many opportunities that this attitude (do we call it *too cool for shul?*) misses, and that Friedman does not, are the wicked humor that can arise only from a fair fight with a formidable antagonist. Like Saul Bellow, Friedman raises the stakes and thereby, paradoxically, makes the jokes funnier.

Fire Year is crowded with true lovers—of God, of music, of art, of the body. Friedman doesn't build a hedge around them. He subjects their love to the test of experience. In "There's Hope for Us All," the world's only expert on an obscure Renaissance painter is so wedded to her view of the painter's work, and is so humorless about it, that she denies she has made an interpretation at all. She pleads for lampooning, yet Friedman is too watchful to treat her merely as the object of derision; the vigor of her belief compels, if not his agreement, then at least his close attention. "Interpretation kills!" she insists, sort of ridiculously. But isn't she sort of right?

The book is full of wonderful moments of compressed and earnest hope, mixed with an affectionate humor that somehow works not by distancing you from the character—the better to sneer at him—but by bringing you closer to his plight. The critic James Wood calls this "the humor of forgiveness." In "All the World's a Field," one man dreams of a new life for his family in America: "They would keep goats and chickens and meditate on Torah near the stillness of cows, and they would feel God's presence wherever they went." You do not laugh at this man, as though Friedman had made a fool of him; you laugh at yourself for having failed to see that such a modest goal could hold out such grand promise.

Throughout these stories Friedman takes to heart the advice commonly attributed to Ford Madox Ford: if a character appears in a story long enough to sell a newspaper, the writer ought to make him real enough that we can smell his breath. Even the passersby bear the writer's closest look. Memorable figures abound: a rich, married, Southern Protestant, bi-curious alpha male; Orthodox Jews living in Georgia plantation manses; a vain, middlebrow museum curator closeted to no one but himself; an otherwise kosher-keeping woman with a passion for hush puppies fried in the same oil as shrimp—each of these characters might have been played for caricature when you consider the unlikelihood of their cohabiting in the same stories. But there are no dramatic *types* here, only people. Even when they appear for just a flash, Friedman makes a whole character out of one brisk stroke. An old man with tufted dirty hair growing out of his ears inspires not disgust for his dishevelment, but tenderness. A security guard asks a gay associate curator about his home life: "Out of the two of y'all, who the one cooks?" A widow summarizes her husband with the bristling epitaph: "She knew only that he had not died one second before the last breath left his body— every second of his life he had lived!"

By the resounding conclusion of the final story, you will be wide awake to the rigors and the dangers of belief; the vertigo of losing it; and the holy terror of laughing. Candid, cunning, brave, and wickedly funny—*Fire Year* will make you remember the first time you read Philip Roth. Here you'll find love, lust, religious tradition, the new South, the transcendent promise of faith, the liberating hope of sexual awakening; Friedman twists them all into stories as true to our goofy joys as to our deepest intuitions.

—Salvatore Scibona

FIRE YEAR

Blue

The adults had been there for hours—the ones from out of town, for days—and they all seemed happy, huddled in little groups that opened up whenever I passed, to let me in. They were offering me a space to receive their congratulations and slurred life advice. I smiled gamely and kept walking through my grandparents' house—through the sunroom, past the living room picture window, past the silver platters of food, the crystal decanters with little nametags chained around their necks. I had nowhere to go. I had changed out of my bar mitzvah suit into an aqua leisure suit with a polyester shirt depicting a crowded seafloor scene. I had blow-dried and sprayed my hair into a kind of helmet. I was ready for someone my age to show up. I was ready for a miracle to take place and a cool bar mitzvah party to assemble on the screened back porch. A bar mitzvah was, after all, a religious celebration, and in those days it was religion alone that lifted me out of despair, inspiring in me the fervid hope that everything would be all right.

I happened to be in the foyer to witness the spectacle of Aaron Elkins making his entrance. It was July, it was Savannah, my grandparents' air conditioner had broken, and so the attic fan was on. I stood in the insuck of hot air through the open front door and watched Aaron navigate his way up the criss-cross redbrick walkway. Massive cockroaches illuminated in the front porch lights flew across his path, causing him to skip and dodge and do a minstrel-like little dance. At one point his hands shot up and his palms pressed against the sides of his head. Aaron was a fellow regular at the first table by the steps in the lunchroom pit. He had been born a blue baby and struck me as a puny and contemptible figure, but I was glad he had come.

"There's about a million cockroaches out there." Aaron had stopped on the front porch and was wiping his forehead with a shredded Kleenex. The corners of his purple mouth tilted down in a textbook frown, his shoulders were hunched, his entire physical presentation reflecting the effort it took him to get there. "Nine hundred ninety-nine thousand still alive. I stomped about a thousand of them. Oh, unless they've been doing it." He leered at me as he stood there catching his breath. "Then there'd be more of them than when I got here. Have you ever seen two gigantic flying cockroaches doing it?"

"Come in," I said, taking a deep breath. This was only my first guest. I had an entire night to endure.

"Are there any girls here yet?" he asked, stepping under the fanlight, his yellow eyes aglow from the blazing chandelier.

"You've got pieces of Kleenex stuck to your forehead," I said.

He raked his skin with his long bluish nails, then did his version of a grin. "Which girls did you invite?"

"All of them."

"Leslie Lee?" he asked.

"I said all of them."

"Oo, Leslie Lee," he said dreamily, his eyes closing. Then he opened them and grabbed ahold of an invisible pair of skinny hips, pulling them into his groin three times as he goat-ishly intoned each syllable of her last name: "Des-Bouil-lons."

"Come on," I said, looking around, in case anyone had seen.

I took him through the kitchen.

"You look like you're about to cry," he said from behind.

In the kitchen the two maids, my grandparents' and ours, looked up from the trays of hors d'oeuvres they were arranging and smiled simultaneously. This struck me as a kind and classy gesture for which I felt absurdly grateful. My mother was giving them orders from against the kitchen sink and ignored me.

My luck ran out in the dining room. Everyone was engaged talking with someone else except for Harry Sandman, my godfather, who was standing at the window looking out at the garden. The other men wore coats and ties but he had on a striped sports shirt and a pair of slacks, as if to call attention to his bachelorhood and confirm all the rumors. The reason he lived in a carriage house downtown, an aunt had once said, was to be closer to the "whores he ran with." The carriage house was a block away from the auto-repair garage he owned, but this was apparently a secondary convenience. He turned just as I passed behind him, pinning Aaron and me to the dining room table.

His hairline started very high on his head; below that, he had a deep reddish tan and spots like watermelon seeds here and there. "Ho, ho, the bar mitzvah boy! Look at that shirt, that's a voyage to the bottom of the sea." He put his arm around me, then stuck out the other one toward Aaron. "Harry Sandman, glad to meet you."

"__ __"

"Did you know I held this kid in my hands?"

Aaron shook his head, and it was unclear whether he meant yes or no.

"I had his legs spread as wide as I could, I was holding down his fat little calves—this kid was a kicker! One wrong move and he'd have been a little girl! Do you follow me?"

Aaron laughed at this.

"Who's your daddy?" Harry asked.

"Simon Elkins."

"Simon Elkins I've known since he was a boy. Tell him hello. Tell him to bring his car into the garage for a checkup. On the house, free of charge. What is it, a black Dodge Dart station wagon, '69, '70?"

"Sixty-nine, heh-heh," Aaron said, recognizing a kindred spirit.

Harry looked at him for a second, then broke into a smile. "Your friend's got a dirty mind," he said into my face. "And one hell of a tan."

"Well, we better get to the porch," I said.

"I like that in a boy." I was wondering if Harry meant the dirty mind or the tan when he kissed me on the lips. He tasted of pickles and booze. "I like you too. This is a hell of a party you're throwing. I think there are more people here than came to the thing this morning. Hey, Aaron, did you hear how this kid reads Hebrew, like a professional?"

"Yeah," Aaron said sourly, "he read it for three hours straight."

Harry considered this. "He did read for three hours straight, didn't he?"

"It sure seemed like it if he didn't."

"It was a double parsha," I said in my defense.

But I didn't feel defensive. I had known what I was doing. The moon's position in the sky accounted for why a double portion needed to be read from the Torah that day, but I alone was responsible for the hours of uninterrupted, practically tuneless Hebrew chanting coming off the altar. The cantor, my bar mitzvah coach, had suggested we do excerpts of the two long readings; a little here, a little there, then on to something else. I said we'd do it the way God wrote it, and it wasn't a medley. The cantor, who'd escaped a Polish labor camp, run through a hundred nights, eaten the soles of his shoes, sighed. No one stands there for more than two hours straight reading from the Torah, he pointed out, especially at our middle-of-the-road synagogue, which prided itself on not being crazy liberal but not being crazy Orthodox either. In addition, he said, to paraphrase his elegant accented English, reading the two sections in their entirety and in Hebrew would bore the shit out of the congregation. I knew he was right but I would not be swayed. To keep us on some kind of schedule we had cut out my today-I-am-a-man speech, we had cut out the rabbi's talk, we had cut out the part where the zaftig Elizabeth Taylor–esque Sisterhood president, Mrs. Glass, hands me a silver cup— we had cut out everything that could possibly be considered entertainment at a bar mitzvah.

The day came and I stood there reading the ancient words, feeling God's breath rise from my lungs and pass through my lips, and occasionally looking up and registering the emptying sanctuary. The endless lines of unpunctuated consonants, some of them crowned, rose and seemed to hover above the parchment, the letters black and watery but crisp-edged, and when I looked up I couldn't make out faces, only the movement of bodies toward the door. At first they left one at a time, pretending to go to the bathroom or have a smoke. Then they left in pairs. And then, abandoning all shame, they left in groups of three and four and more. I looked up for the last time when I was nearing the end, the part where the Hebrews, camped on the far side of the Jordan, within sight of the Holy Land, listen to Moses relay God's commandments on whom their daughters may marry. The front two rows were still filled with family, zombie-eyed and dutiful, but the rest of the sanctuary was empty save for an odd man here and there, like the audience at a midnight showing of a Czechoslovakian animated film. I didn't know where the rest of the guests had gone, but they all reappeared in the social hall when it was time to eat.

Beethoven's *Emperor* Concerto was playing on the stereo, white tapers columned in glass rose from every surface, bowls of hydrangeas lay among the platters of food. Then we crossed over onto the porch, where the kids' party was still waiting to begin. The cement floor was painted red and it seemed to change color throughout the day; now, under the bare bulb, it looked like one great field of rust. It was a little sandy under our shoes. Lizards were mounted at various levels on the outside of the screen, and Aaron observed their undersides with uncharacteristic silence. Moths crashed wildly into the screen, and the only sound you heard was the crickets.

I walked over to the stack of singles by the record player. "Moonlight Feels Right," "Afternoon Delight," "Dream Weaver"—I had bought them all last weekend at Kmart.

Aaron turned away from the lizards. "Are you going to play a record?"

"Okay." I put on "Love Will Keep Us Together."

"Who do you think the first girl's going to be?" he asked when the song was over.

"I don't know."

"Come on, guess. Leslie Lee?"

"Maybe."

"What if no girls show up?"

I figured somebody had to say it eventually.

"Hello." It was Mark Cohen, standing in the doorway

between the sunroom and the porch. Instinctively I held my breath. He did not smell bad but sometimes I gagged when I saw him—an inconvenient reflex, because he was another of the guys who ate lunch at the first table in the pit. One morning at Jewish day camp Mark shat in his bathing suit. We were five years old. We were lined up for roll call and I was standing behind him. He was as disgusted as the rest of us—he slipped out of his yellow trunks and ran naked into the building. From then on even the name Mark Cohen carried with it the smell of shit.

Aaron covered his nose and mouth with his palms and moved away from the doorway, saying the muffled word "gasmask" over and over, proving, as if there had been any doubt, that a comradeship of outcasts is no comradeship at all.

"Happy bar mitzvah." Mark handed me a long slim box. "I got you a belt. You can take it back if you don't like it."

This was something about Mark—he was as sweet as the memory he conjured was foul.

"Thanks," I said. "You should get something to drink. There's ginger ale and punch."

"I think I'll get some punch. Do you want some?"

Mark went out and Aaron took my elbow and said, "Come over here."

"What? Why?"

"Come on."

When we got to the corner he said, "Do you know what you looked like up there?"

"Up where?"

"At the synagogue. Reading from the Torah."

I shook my head.

"You were swaying."

"You're supposed to do that."

"Yeah, but you looked like you meant it."

I shrugged.

"You're taking yourself off in a very extreme direction."

"I am not."

"And your suit pants are highwaters."

I glared at him, insisting he come to the point.

"No girl is ever going to like you like that," he finally said.

Standing on the altar swaying, like a tree blown by the spirit of the Lord—I had meant it. My religious awakening occurred just a few months before, at Mama Leone's restaurant in New York. It was night three of my eighth-grade trip.

Night one: hurtling north through darkness on Amtrak's *Silver Star*, Tally McPherson slipping across the aisle to sit with Leslie Lee Desbouillons, Sara Bousquet giving up her seat to sit with Chip Spenser, a car full of adolescents as beautiful as their names coupling in the darkness, silent against the noises of the night, the hypnotic chug-a-chut of the wheels, the lonely call of the whistle at the intersections of county roads, the snoring of the chaperones—the landscape of sound that I traveled through, that the lovers surely didn't notice. Night two: in a grotesque twist, the TV in the room I shared with Aaron Elkins hadn't been blocked from showing adult movies, and so the entire class, sixty horny kids, piled onto the beds and the carpet watching *Confessions of a Window Cleaner*. This was the happiest night of Aaron's life and he wasn't even watching the movie. Neither was I. The window cleaner was skinny and smooth-skinned and he had a huge dick, but if I looked anywhere in the direction of the screen I was sure the entire class would notice my fascination. That night I lay listening to Aaron's rubbing against the sheets, his pitiful moans, wondering if these sad exertions would kill him.

By night three I was, apparently, ready to accept God's salvation. A plate of veal parmesan was placed before me. Meat and milk in combination was forbidden, I had learned in Hebrew school, though we ate it all the time at home: veal parmesan, cheeseburgers, beef stroganoff . . . The chaperones had selected a five-course meal for us. My choice was whether to eat at all. But it didn't seem like a conscious decision. It was more like when Pharaoh tested the baby Moses with two piles, one of gold coins and the other of steaming coals, and if he chose the gold, he would be put to death. Naturally, he reached for the coins, but at the last moment an angel averted his hand and he touched a coal. His burnt finger flew up to his mouth, singeing his tongue, permanently impeding his speech. My hand didn't burn when I pushed the plate away, but after this silent refusal I barely spoke for the rest of the trip.

Dennis Hornstein sprinted from the far end of the living room to the foyer, then out the front door. He had been running in and out all night and my grandparents were furious, which seemed to me some measure of my party's success. It was not exactly wild but there had been surprises. All the guys from the loser table in the lunchroom had shown up and so had a few others whom no one could consider losers—Dennis, who was actually going out with someone, was one of them.

I wasn't exactly happy but I knew it could be worse. Aaron knew no such thing—he had one measure of success and his count of girls remained at zero. When Dennis showed up on the back porch again, still out of breath, Aaron cornered him and demanded to know where his girlfriend, Karen Karesh, was.

"She didn't come," Dennis said.

"Duh," Aaron said. "Why didn't she come?"

"Uh, I don't know."

"Did you ask her?"

"She knew I was coming but she didn't want to come."

"Well, why not?"

He shook his head.

"Don't move," Aaron said, going into the sunroom. He came back with a phone trailing a cord. "Call her."

"He doesn't have to call," I pleaded. Did I really want to know why someone wouldn't come to my party?

"I already talked to her today," Dennis said.

"Give him a break," I said.

"Call her and ask her why she isn't here," Aaron insisted.

Dennis shrugged and dialed. Two little moths had gotten onto the porch, and as he waited he watched their little suicide flights into the bulb. I lifted the needle, silencing "Bohemian Rhapsody."

"Hey," Dennis said softly into the receiver.

"Ask her," Aaron said.

"Uh, hey," Dennis said in a normal voice. "Do you want to come over?" He looked at us as he listened, then looked back at the phone when it was his turn to talk. "Is it fun? Kind of." He looked at us again, then back at the phone. "Well, why don't you want to come over?"

When he hung up he informed us she didn't think there would be any girls there.

Aaron made two loose fists and pounded them against his own head.

"Aaron," I said.

"Aaahhhhhh!" he said, still pounding.

"Stop it," I said. "You're going to hurt yourself."

"I hate girls." He dropped to one knee and rested his elbow on the other one, gently panting. "How can there be any girls if no girls show up?"

"I think they're just waiting for someone to go first," Mark said reasonably.

Aaron looked at him and stood up. If he hadn't been such a runt, he would have been right in Mark's face. I thought Aaron was going to lunge. Instead he said, "What's your sister doing tonight?"

"I don't know," Mark said. "Nothing."

"You don't know or she's doing nothing? Which is it?"

"Sally's eleven years old," I said when I realized what Aaron was doing.

He picked up the phone, which had somehow got set down in the middle of the floor, and said, "Call her."

"All right," Mark replied.

Sally came over. She was wearing white shorts and a frilly white blouse and I think she'd done something with her eyes—the lashes appeared to have been greased and somehow separated. She sat in the center of the room, under the bulb, on a beach chair with the back frayed into a hole the size of a grapefruit. It was the best of the lot we found stacked against the wall. She sat on this throne without a trace of self-consciousness. There was something uncanny about her. She was an eleven-year-old girl but she sat there with the air of an adult, of her mother specifically, I suppose. She hadn't been tainted by her brother's reputation. She crossed her legs and maintained a constant smile and didn't seem to mind that everyone kept running past or around her and no one even looked her way. We pretended she wasn't there—but she was the blank space that defined the walls around it, the absence around which everything we wanted was gathered.

"Would you like something to drink?" I finally asked.

"I would, thank you kindly."

"We have ginger ale and punch."

"I believe I'll try the punch," she replied, folding her hands in her lap.

In the sunroom a cherub forming the stem of a lamp listened with his head cocked to a conch shell. A lightbulb rose from his curls and cast a warm puddle of light on the Oriental rug. A two-foot marble reproduction of the *David* stood on a pedestal in the corner. It was a house full of wonders and flowers and music and light. And adults so intensely engaged with one another, so lost in their merry drunkenness, that by this point in the evening they had stopped opening up their circles, given up congratulating me.

There were exceptions. Sympathetic souls like my grandmother. I had last seen her scolding Dennis for running through her house, and now, propped against the Knabe baby grand with a tumbler of bourbon in her hand, she smiled at me—she didn't blame me for the wildness of my friends. My uncle Ben, who was recently divorced and now took me as his date to the symphony, stood by the mahogany radio console, which glowed from its deep polish, and winked at me so discreetly that discretion itself seemed the point of the gesture. He was signaling that we wouldn't talk or even acknowledge each other—but he wanted me to know he hadn't forgotten about me. In that house full of people we could share this moment completely unnoticed, no one but us could know the depth of our connection—and it was all right. This seemed to me then to have something to do with becoming an adult.

And yet it wasn't enough, none of it was enough. What was wrong with me! The crumminess of my party on the porch was clear to me, as was the elegance and warmth of the party in here—but I didn't belong at either of them. Dennis and Mark raced past me. Where were they going? How did they know where to go? We were no longer children, we didn't just run around and around for no reason at all. But my friends were always describing some orbit in the house or outside. The adults standing in their circles were also revolving, slowly, so that when I passed back through the sunroom with Sally's punch, the people whose backs had been to me were now facing me, though still they paid me no mind.

I stood on the threshold between the house and the back porch. "I Honestly Love You" was playing out there. Under the now-dark bulb Aaron and Sally were holding each other and standing in place, leaning in one direction for a while, then in the other. Aaron was barely taller than she. Their hands were pressed deeply into each other's backs. Their eyes were closed. The chair had been pushed over to the side. Nobody else was on the porch but them—and me. It had gotten a little cooler and the attic fan seemed less useless, so that instead of a rush of hot air you were standing in a breeze. Now that the light was off, you could make out the camellia and hydrangea bushes beyond the screen. Moonlight silvered the tops of the power lines and from someone's yard a dog barked.

From Rameses they came, from Succoth, from Etham, from Marah. They came from Elim, from the Red Sea, from the wilderness of Sin. They came from Dophkah, from Alush, from waterless Rephidim. From the Sinai wilderness, from Rimmon-perez, from Libnah they came. From Rissah, from Kehelath, from Mount Shepher, from Haradah. They started in Egypt and stopped in dozens of places lacking everything but a name. Every destination also a place of departure, every *from* also a *to*—but only provisionally. They were always leaving. It is the final destination alone that matters, the encampments along the way dutifully recorded but usually without a syllable of description, nothing to impede the way to Canaan, every place a stone in a desert riprap over which the human stream can swiftly pour—but also a piece of a caravan fixed in place in the sacred text, with one end in Egypt and the other always in the Holy Land.

And then the people stop moving. Sitting on the wrong bank of the Jordan, they listen to Moses tell them what God has in store for them, what they are commanded to do and what they are forbidden. And this is where the reading ends.

A cliffhanger. But everyone knows what happens. They get where they're going. They fulfill their destiny.

It had not been so long since my Mama Leone's conversion. Just enough time for me to learn the Torah portion. I had read the translation maybe once. I hardly knew what I was saying but I didn't care—it was an ecstatic experience I was after, I wanted to lose myself quite literally. And yet somehow up there, reading the chain of untranslatable place names, things made a kind of sense to me. Sense—I tried to get it to go away. The words rose from the parchment and I would not let them settle, I poured myself into the letters, confined myself in their shapes. It didn't work. Chanting the place names, I identified with the Hebrews on their journey, I was on the journey myself. My adolescent egotism disgusted me; it was banal, foreclosing ecstasy, trapping me in myself. In my department-store suit I was there in Rephidim, in Kehelath, in Tahath, in Terah—and I wondered how I could possibly believe I was going anywhere, much less making progress to a land of milk and honey. Just because some guy who had conversations with God said so? I was fleeing slavery but into what? How could I believe I would ever escape that endless chain of bumfuck towns—the Vidalia and Valdosta of the desert, the Elabelle, Eulolia, Cordelia, Waycross. Savannah. The towns were bad enough—were they even towns, or just bunches of palms in the desert?—but how to have faith on the shores of the Red Sea or in the middle of barren wilderness? Endless pineforest and marsh surrounded Savannah on three sides, the ocean on the other—but why resort to analogies when it was the wilderness of myself from which there was no escape?

I was thinking about all this as I stood there in the darkness watching Aaron and Sally dance. Something had to happen, didn't it?

The song ended. They didn't pull apart. The string to the

bulb hung behind Sally's back and I went over and snapped the light on. Aaron opened his eyes and smiled at me over her shoulder. I smiled miserably back. His forearms were crossed on her back, his palms pressed into her. He didn't let go. The bottoms of his hands remained firmly planted. But the tops of them inclined slowly away from her, his hands swiveled on his wrists, his thumbs flexed. He was giving me a double thumbs-up.

He would be dead in three years. He must have known it. He reached over and pulled the string, he squeezed her to his chest and they swayed to a music you could almost hear.

Reunion

Sing to me, Muse, of why anyone would attend their high school reunion. I'm not talking about those people who liked high school, who peaked in their senior year. What about the rest of us, the queers, the dykes, the pansies, the fags, the fruits, the freaks, the punks, the goths, the dreamers, the losers, the tortured, the confused, the spazzes, the nerds, the dorks, the fatties, the brains, the potheads, the poets, the painfully shy—there are more of us than there were of them. *Reunion.* Break it down into its parts, watch how it decomposes into nonsense phones: *ree-YOON-yun.* The punchline of a Borscht Belt joke at the expense of the Chinese. A reunion, to reune, to reunite—why, we were never united to begin with, we comrades in sorrow. We've kept in touch with those of our fellow misfits we've wanted to keep in touch with, and besides, they wouldn't go to the reunion either.

And so when Zora, my best friend from those days, asked me if I was going to our twenty-fifth high school reunion, I laughed into the phone.

"We'll show up together in black leather, looking fabulous," she envisioned.

"We can just do that somewhere downtown," I pointed out.

"Yes, but back home we'll look so much better—relatively."

"Look, I don't want to go."

"But it'll be fun, love."

"Actually, it won't be. It'll be a trial."

"Maybe," she conceded. "But sometimes people are tried. That's life. That's history. It isn't always nice."

"How about I take you out for an expensive lunch?"

"Because I want you to come with me to our reunion."

"Okay," I said, giving in.

In fact I would have done anything for her, because on our senior prom night she had done me a favor. I had a girlfriend, from the class below us, whom I had been trying to get rid of for months. She wanted what I couldn't give and yet she remained deaf to my coded entreaty, "It's not you, really it's not!" It was the best I could do at the time but it wasn't working. Zora didn't have a date to the prom. This was the cruel fate of a foreign-born girl with razor-sharp cheekbones and the year-book quote "Of all that I love, I love most that which has been written in blood." She showed up near the end of the evening and the three of us left together. Ollie Byrd was red-cheeked and slight and Zora dispatched her in a two-step drinking contest: tequila shots at a Mexican place on Hartley Extension, notorious for serving the underaged, followed by ramekins of maple-flavored corn syrup at our local 24-hour Christian diner. I laid Ollie Byrd out on the backseat and touched two fingers to her neck. Then we drove to the beach, where Zora and I sat smoking on the hood of the car and watched the sun rise and glimpsed the possibility of a less pathetic life.

Since then Zora's homeland had ceased to exist and she herself had mostly disappeared, somewhere on the Lower East Side. I moved to New York too, to Chelsea, where I had a group of friends, got laid regularly, held a steady job, and enjoyed the sort of nice life that Zora apparently scorned. Whenever I ran into her we promised to set a date to meet—but we never did. And now that she had called me, my beloved Zora, *this* was what she wanted to propose?

I bought a ticket to the reunion. I bought a nonrefundable flight. I notified my family. The weekend before, I called Zora to confirm and plan outfits. It turned out she was getting back together with her man and she didn't want to leave town at such a delicate point in their relationship. Besides, he was insanely jealous, even of her gay friend. I understood, didn't I?

"You're sending me down there by myself," I said.

"I'm sorry!" she said, a little desperately. "I didn't plan it this way. I wouldn't want to go down there by myself either!"

She wanted me to understand that she sympathized with me and that this decision of hers wasn't premeditated—that I wasn't, in short, the Ollie Byrd of this situation. But somehow this failed to console.

In the following week I got two emails. The first was from someone named Winson Kingsley. He identified himself as Tag from our high school class and wrote, "Hey, Edward, wanna get together when you're in town for Reunion?" He didn't explain how he had gone from Tag to Winson or why he was asking to get together, and so familiarly too. We had gone through middle school and high school together without exchanging a single word.

Tag was a rich kid who played football and baseball, he may have been the captain of one or both teams, he wore a jacket with a letter on it, he was a terrible student. But unlike your typical jock, he was chatty, at least with his friends. From a distance I could see the verve with which he expressed himself; he talked with his face and his hands, his entire body. He acted in school plays, he sang, and sometimes, I heard, he went to the woods at the edge of campus to smoke.

But Tag's place in the class's imagination owed less to these standard biographical facts than to an unusual one: the hirsuteness of his legs. They were so nice and hairy that they inspired a corresponding admiration among the other boys in the class. Rumors flew: Some short-skirted girl from a rival school had come simply by sitting in his lap. The legs were the sign of a virility so great that he himself could come several times in a night, even after drinking a jug of Boone's Farm strawberry wine. I was so tortured by shame and confusion—I wasn't certain I even knew what it meant to come—that I didn't dare give in to these fantasies, and in fact the only time I ever took a good look at those legs was when everyone else was looking at them too. It was a pep rally, and from the safety of the bleachers I watched Tag come out in his girlfriend's wraparound skirt, his fur-tufted hooves stuffed into her pink espadrilles. Everyone sure pepped up at that, everyone but me. Struck by this display of manly beauty in a female setting—I believe he might even have sashayed—I sat there as still as a corpse.

It had been decades since I last thought about him. And so his invitation made me feel nothing more than mild curiosity. Typing those four letters—*Sure*—was surprisingly easy to do.

The other email was from my brother, Ray. He came from an altogether different realm than Tag. He didn't drink, didn't smoke, never smiled, planned on getting rich. Real estate was his field, though he seemed to have no knack for it. He resembled the biblical brothers, the murderers, the tricksters—except he was inept and couldn't murder, couldn't trick. Over the years he had nursed numerous grievances against me—the love of his life had dumped him after I revealed some secret; hard liquor nauseated him because I had forced it on him as a kid—but he couldn't get any of these charges to stick. Back then he had other tormentors too, classmates of his who occasionally dragged him out onto the playground and beat him. But he wouldn't squeal and he even came back for more, waiting silently and blackly on the sidelines, staring out at nothing.

I saw the martyr's look in his eyes, though I only witnessed him being beaten once. I was in the lunchroom reading, and the headmaster, whose office was next door, popped his head out and asked me to deliver a note to his wife, the physics teacher. On my way I noticed a commotion at the far end of the quad, and Ray turned out to be at the center of it. There were three boys from his class taking turns pounding him, and as I ran up to them they stopped what they were doing and started laughing at me, the boy the headmaster chose, the boy he always chose, to deliver a message to his wife. My brother, his head twisted at a heartbreaking angle, looked up and started laughing too.

It was the beatings that got him into karate. I never understood the connection, since I couldn't see him relinquishing his dark power by fighting back. But at the age of forty he was still competing. In his email he told me, in a bluff tone he had at some point picked up, that he was in a tournament the day before the reunion and that I should come check it out, dude! I didn't see why I should come check it out. I didn't even email him back. Then he emailed me again, and this time I thought, *Oh, what could it hurt?*

The tournament took place in the long cinderblock building where my brother trained. Inside the door were two flags, American and Confederate. The coach's wife stood behind a table with Cokes, chips, and an iced lemon cake. About fifty spectators milled around and took their seats.

The coach, a deeply tanned man with buzzed white hair, nodded at me and looked away.

Southerners' reputation for hospitality is overstated. This phenomenon of people I had known for much of my life nodding and looking away from me whenever I was back in town was more familiar. What happened since I moved away? I came out. Before that, everyone may have suspected, but because I hadn't yet self-declared, who knows, I might just have been artistic. There was still hope for me, if not to become an active member of heterosexual society, then at least to remain celibate and quiet. Maybe even do something useful in the community, like play the organ at the Lutheran church. Now there was no getting around it: this was a homo they were in close proximity to.

The coach stepped onto the mat. It was his team hosting this event, and his black gi had the same gold insignia on the left breast that was on Ray's white one. He bowed all around and asked for Jesus's blessing.

A towheaded girl of maybe six emerged from a back room and everyone clapped. My brother was small—on the low end of the middleweight category—but in the generational procession unfolding it would be hours before they got to him. The little girl had no opponent. She bowed to the judges—two men and a woman at a folding table against the far wall—and then walked straight backward and bowed again. She went through her routine with care never to break eye contact with the judges or turn her back on them. It was only her final bows that freed her to turn to the audience. She smiled preciously and the crowd went wild.

A short solid man with a blond handlebar mustache appeared. He pointed to the sidelines and said, "How can she row show men meaty!"

Or something like that. Ray had once told me what these commands were and what they meant in English.

Next up for my brother's team was a black kid who looked about twenty and was growing a nice little fro. He had four family members in attendance and they sat off to themselves in the back. His opponent had a breastbone that jutted out like a Ridley Scott reptile.

"Show many ray!" the referee barked and the boys bowed to the judges.

The referee shouted more commands. The boys bowed in various directions in response and then finally began their bouncy little two-steps. The white kid landed a waist-level roundhouse kick and when the black kid rushed him the referee called "Yummy!" and the boys retreated to opposite sides of the mat. The referee said something else and almost immediately the white kid made the same kick. The referee pointed a finger at the black kid but let the fight continue.

Now, rather than rushing his opponent, the black kid danced around him. The white kid kicked but didn't connect and the black kid, fists up, moved straight toward him. The white kid backed up until he had left the mat entirely. The referee started them up again and once more there came the same roundhouse kick, but this time the black kid turned to the referee, wordlessly asking, *How many times are you going to let this white boy kick me in the ass before you let me do something about it?*

Next a big dykey-looking girl with a baby face came out wearing the gi with the gold insignia, and in the back row a wispy guy in a short black trenchcoat started clapping for her.

Finally it was my brother's turn. He never smiled, yet he managed to have a number of expressions anyway—currently it was his down-to-business look. As he zeroed in on his competitor, a mean-looking redhead also approaching middle age, he flashed his athlete-at-peak-performance look, all of his being narrowed to a hot white pinpoint of focus. A vein throbbed in his forehead. He was in the zone and wanted you to know it.

I had hardly gone to any of my brother's competitions, and at those I had attended I focused on the wrong things,

like whether the gi, by concealing so much, didn't in fact erot-
icize what scant flesh it revealed. All I knew was that compared to what had gone before, Ray's match was action packed,
and though the referee never allowed either opponent to even
think about hurting the other, both my brother and the other
guy made a few good combinations of moves. They seemed like
they were fighting, or at least wanted to fight. Ray grunted a lot.

He struck me as the winner. But the judges had penalized
him a point on some technicality that the coach couldn't argue
away, and so Ray finished the tournament in second place.

Afterward, he stuck out a hand and I gave him a hug, more
as a rejection of the handshake than anything else.

"Hey, when'd you get in?" he asked.

"Just now. Came straight here. Congratulations."

"Ah, I should have come in first. Just couldn't get my ki
focused one hundred percent."

"Your key?"

"Hey, you want to meet the guy who won in the heavy-
weight? He's a pretty nice guy."

He was a handsome young man named Ramirez who had
a little gold cross around his neck. "This is my brother," Ray
said. "He just got in from New York City." Ray looked me up
and down. "Black must be in fashion up there. Or maybe he's
attending a funeral after this, heh-heh, heh-heh."

"I love New York," Ramirez said.

"That's what they say," I said.

"I happen to like Sarah Palin," my brother said. "They'd
probably think I was an idiot up in New York City, wouldn't
they?"

"I don't think you're really on their radar," I replied.

"But let's say for example that I did go up there and started
telling everyone how much I liked Sarah Palin, they'd think I
was an idiot, don't you think?"

"Uh, maybe," I said.

"Definitely," he said.

"Well, now that you mention it," I said.

"See?" he concluded. "Now let's go, bro, I'm starving."

He took me to a sports bar with about five hundred screens showing various football and basketball games, including a few, judging by the hairstyles and production values, from previous decades. At our table I took a chair with a view of the fewest screens, but my brother remained standing. "We'll get two dozen wings, one hot, one extra-hot," he announced. "I'm telling you, these wings are awesome, especially the extra-hot. You like cayenne pepper, right?"

"I'm a vegetarian," I said.

He winced and frowned at the same time. "Since when?"

"I don't know, since always. I never did like meat."

"But you ate it."

I wondered where this was heading.

"So you're telling me if someone put a medium-rare filet mignon with mushroom-butter-cabernet sauce in front of you," he said with great incredulity, "you wouldn't eat it."

"No, and if Jennifer Lopez shook her naked ass in my face, I wouldn't eat it either."

"Well, I would," he assured me.

One way or another he was trying to connect with me. But I felt nothing for him, not annoyance at being provoked, not nostalgia for an idealized relationship we never had—just nothing at all.

When he wasn't staring at a screen and nibbling on wings, Ray was off working the room. I could see he was considered a nice guy by all. But there was something frantic about his socializing. He handed out cards to everyone he saw. He brought over a guy whose hand he had been ostentatiously pumping and said, "Hey, you remember Kirk."

"Kirk Reichsman," I said. "You were one of the boys who used to beat the shit out of my little brother."

Kirk shook my hand and nodded. He was giving me that got-a-homo-in-my-face look, wary but curious.

"Are you still at your place on Lafayette?" my brother asked him. "That house next door to you sell yet? Who was it that moved in, do you know? I think we need to get you behind a gate. You live in a beautiful house, don't get me wrong, I wouldn't tell you I could sell it for you if I didn't believe in its showability, not to mention its salability, myself." He pulled out a card.

How had Ray changed since school? He had barely graduated from State, he hadn't made any money, he still lived with our parents, for God's sake. He had nothing now but a flat stomach and a shelf full of karate medals as armor, apparently never wondering if they were enough to make up for the past. Maybe that was the point of all the noise—not to have to hear himself wondering.

After Kirk left, Ray said, "You know, I never meet people like you, bro, so I find it interesting to hear your opinions."

I sighed.

"I meet a lot of people in my line of business that are armed and want to form a militia to overthrow the government," he said, matter-of-factly, as if his line of work involved staging houses for Al-Qaeda. "But I tell them just go out and vote. That's what you do if you don't like the way things are going in this country."

He wanted me to know that down here he was considered a moderate.

"I too believe it's better to vote than to form a militia and overthrow the government," I replied.

He snickered, showing he hadn't lost all perspective.

"So I'm playing the reunion," he said.

"My reunion? You still have a band?"

"It's a paid gig," he said, shrugging. "But I do it just as a hobby."

He had started playing bass and singing in a band around the time he took up karate. Just a bunch of guys he knew, practicing in the garage, playing grimly faithful covers of Southern-rock classics. If they ever had a gig, I never heard about it. Ray put up posters of the Rolling Stones and the Allman Brothers on his walls; my tastes ran to Donna Summer and Queen. It was hopeless even back then.

Now that Ray had brought it up, I imagined the reunion in all its horror, one hour stretching into the next and the next and the next.

"What are you doing tonight?" he asked.

"Going to the Boat Club with Tag Kingsley."

He gave me a classic look of this-does-not-compute. "You? Why?"

His head was cocked at a strange angle and I could see his face looking at me from underneath that pile of boys. It was the same look, without the laugh, that he was giving me now.

"I didn't know y'all kept in touch," he said.

"We haven't."

"I didn't know y'all even talked to each other."

"We didn't."

"Then what the hell?"

For once my brother and I were thinking the same thing. And it wasn't just that Tag and I didn't really know each other. It was also that Ray and I weren't members of the Boat Club, our parents weren't in society and would never have been asked to join. I felt uneasy about setting foot there, but when we made our email plans Tag told me not to worry, it wasn't the place it used to be.

"I've been trying to make inroads at the Boat Club," my brother said. "That's how business deals are done in this town, over shrimp cocktails and bourbon and gingers. I hear they do an appetizer that's oysters two ways, one raw and the other baked with bacon and a little grated Asiago cheese. Topped with breadcrumbs. I've been trying to get myself sponsored to join, at least get invited there for lunch. Maybe I'll come with you."

His want was so naked, his knowledge of the menu so detailed, that I was almost tempted to invite him along.

I loitered just inside the door. The place was shadowy and deserted, mute and heavily decorated, like a rich neighborhood. I had forgotten the Club was on a river until I glimpsed it through a row of portholes cut into the dark wood. Scraps of dull light lay on the water but the marsh had lost its color. I looked at my watch—it was a little early but well within the dinner hour. No one was around.

"Edward!" Tag said. "What are you doing here in the coatroom?"

Did he think I'd ever been here before?

"You look great!" he said.

"So do you, Tag. Or am I supposed to call you Winson?"

He grinned. "That is my name, you know. I don't know how that damn *Tag* got started. Something about a game of tag."

His hair was sprinkled with gray, he had a soft little bulge around his middle, but he was still sexy. He was wearing the same clothes he had worn before—khakis and a light-blue button-down shirt. He had on Topsiders without socks and I could see his dark hairy ankles, like the thing you wake up with that proves you weren't dreaming.

Tag sat us at a table looking onto a jumble of yachts. A gray-haired black waiter in a white jacket came over and handed us two big laminated menus and took our drink orders. Tag put his menu down and took something out of his pocket: a squarish piece of foil, flat around the edges, with a little oblong bump in the middle.

"It's good to see you," he said. "I read on your profile that you live up in New York. That must make you feel so great."

"Actually it does. But you know, it's just where I live."

"You always did things your own way. I admired that."

From time to time Zora and I met up with some former classmate who had landed in New York, some lost soul who had strayed from the predetermined path—college in the South; marriage to someone from the school; a big house in the same neighborhood he or she grew up in; a kid enrolled at the school—but couldn't find another path to embark on. It was impressive how far some of these people had strayed—one summer the Pep Club president, stabilized on antidepressants, showed up. They sought us out, Zora and me, as bohemians who had succeeded in finding another way.

Tag, sitting here so proprietarily, was obviously not of their kind. But he wanted me to understand that although he'd stayed in town, he hadn't followed the expected path either. His father owned all the luxury-car dealerships in town and Tag was supposed to take them over one day. Instead he had opened an eco-friendly architecture firm with his wife, who not only was from out of town but was Jewish as well.

"How long has it been since I've seen you?" he asked.

Have you ever seen me? I wanted to ask. But I wasn't nervous. I could feel the full force of me, this person I had become, filling the space of my body, who-I-was-now totally eclipsing who-I-was-then.

"I guess it's been around twenty-five years." But I couldn't keep this up as if it were normal. "Tag, did we ever really hang out before?"

"No!" he said, his eyes lighting up.

The waiter came by. Tag ordered a shrimp cocktail and a steak and another martini. I opened the menu. There were no prices on it. The vegetarian options were a salad and I quickly settled on it.

"I'm glad you said that, because we didn't hang out!" Tag went on. "And that's exactly why I wanted to meet you here today. Because people don't hang out with people that are different. I was just talking about this with Susan today. Did my parents even know any Jews? I mean, come on, now, what's the big deal, y'all!"

This incoherent speech was strangely charming, and I could see why he had been so popular. "Then what are we doing here?" I asked.

"Well, that's just it. They've embraced my wife here, and she's just as Jewish as they come. Would you believe they've started to get a challah bread delivered from up north along with the lobsters and they keep it just for her, for when we come in on a Friday night? The kids love it too."

"Is your wife a member or is she just covered under your plan?" I asked.

"This isn't a health clinic," he said, frowning. "And yes, we do have a family membership. But the point is she's the first Jewish person. And now, I mean, one thing can lead to another and—"

I waited. He flicked the little foil packet back and forth, the way we used to do with paper footballs when we were kids.

"This thing, this thing," he said. "I mean, it's gone on for too long."

Whatever it was he was talking about, he kept saying "this thing" and I kept looking at the crumpled foil, and the association between foil and thing was soon complete in my mind. I wanted to know what was inside, and if there was nothing,

I wanted to unfold its thousand surfaces and flatten it into legibility.

"I mean," he went on, "there are no gay members of the Boat Club. Come on now, the time has come!"

And so the thing had a specific meaning, it wasn't just the mystery of the past.

"I doubt there aren't any gay members of the Boat Club," I said.

"Really?" he asked, leaning in with a do-tell look.

"Oh, my God," I said. "You want to sponsor me to join the Boat Club."

"Do it, man, do it. You love it as an idea, I can tell."

"Yes, it's absolute genius. I live hundreds of miles away and I don't own a boat, so nobody would ever have to run into me in the lockerroom or anywhere else for that matter."

He frowned. "It's actually super-competitive to get in, you know. We know people that've been asking us for, like, generations to sponsor them. I can't believe you aren't interested."

It was a relief from the strange normalcy of our conversation, glimpsing the entitled prince peeking out from behind his welcoming mask.

"You really can't believe that I personally am not interested?"

"Well, I guess I can."

I smiled at him meaningfully. "You're very nice to ask. Thank you."

"Okay." He finished off his second martini. "So are you looking forward to the reunion tomorrow night?"

He had accepted my refusal so easily, I felt wounded. Wasn't he even going to beg a little?

He was not. We ate and drank some more and talked about what we had been doing over the last twenty-five years. High school barely came up, as if we had no history and were meeting here for the first time.

Outside, the warm breeze blowing across the river felt good. There's a little fishing community on the bluff, where the river curves under the first bridge from the mainland, and from across the marsh you could see the shrimpboats, strung for some reason with white lights.

"Want to drive to the beach?" he asked. "We're already halfway there."

We took his car, a green Jaguar sportscar. He also had a more practical four-door Mercedes and a Lexus SUV that they used for chauffeuring the kids. (The Kingsleys' eco-friendliness apparently had its limits.) Tag rattled off alphanumeric names of models that meant nothing to me, and as I tried to associate these codes with words I knew—*door, backseat*—I wondered why he was reciting this inventory to me, a carless New Yorker. Cars were the family business but they weren't his business, and when I stopped trying to follow what he was saying I realized he was a little nervous.

I was too. Our dinner had been downright businesslike— he proposed, I declined, no hard feelings, let's have another drink. We were two adults, older and wiser than we had been, the noxiousness of the past mostly gone. But now that I was driving out to the beach with him for no stated reason, a little air started to leak in around the edges of the me who was filling the space of my body, the confident new me I was presenting to Tag. He smelled faintly herbal, a little spicy, like arugula or eucalyptus, and although I had never gotten this close to him, his smell somehow made me aware that I wasn't here with Winson but with Tag, Tag Kingsley, the satyr king toward whom I had shown such deference.

"I used to come out here as a kid," I said, feeling tipsy as we sped across the dark marsh.

"It's nice. I mean, our summer place was in Hilton Head, but it's nice out here too. We used to come here to go parking."

I had gone parking twice with Ollie Byrd, both times total disasters.

Where the main road curved right, running along the ocean side of the island, Tag turned left, toward the river side. No one went to the beach here. The currents were treacherous, and every few years the river spewed raw sewage into the ocean. This part of the island was unfamiliar to me. I couldn't see anything through the trees lining the road, I couldn't even tell if we were driving along the ocean or the river. But soon it felt as if we had gone too far to turn back. Or as if turning back made no sense— only if we kept on could we get back where we started.

We drove past the lighthouse, the one you saw when you were crossing over the bridge to the island. Tag pulled over under an oak tree. We got out and he grabbed a big beach towel from the trunk.

A streetlight marked a little wooden bridge over the dunes, and once we were out of the light's reach it was the moon lighting our way. The waves seemed random and furious, as they always do at night.

Tag laid the towel down on the sand and anchored two corners with his shoes.

Then he started taking off his clothes.

"We aren't going swimming, are we?" I shouted over the wind.

"No, something else." As his pants came off, the little packet of foil came out and he set it down on the towel. "Now, hurry up, I can't stay out all night."

The foil had a condom and a sample-size tube of personal lubricant in it. He handed me the condom. He got down on the towel and squirted some goo into his palm, then he handed the tube to me. How long had he been planning this? A week, twenty-five years? He lay there on his stomach, incredibly still, as if he had gone to sleep or passed out. As if he were dead. My eyes traveled the length of his body, from his toes to the crown

of his head. He had a beautiful back, broad but not too mus-
cular, free of moles and stray hairs. His ass was surprisingly
smooth, as was what I had seen of his chest, and I wondered
if his wife, curled up against him in sleep, dreamed of making
love to an animal or a man.

His legs under mine felt soft and a little springy, like
moss, and I had the sense of plunging into the warmth and the
damp of the earth. I smiled at him in appreciation, though he
couldn't see me. His head was turned to the side but his eyes
were shut tight. If he could have buried his face in the sand, I
sensed, he would have. I myself wasn't going to waste a second
of this by blinking.

I pressed my palms down to steady myself. The sand was
at once hard and unstable. I made fists and tried to balance on
my knuckles, but it didn't help. The towel itself was a joke—
it became instantly heavy with sand and the two unanchored
ends got trapped somewhere beneath us. Sand blew into my
face and everywhere else, and my skin puckered in goose-
bumps. But none of this was much of a distraction. Everything
was proof that this was really happening to me.

Tag seemed to be gritting his teeth. He was making a conscious effort to breathe, and for once in his life he wasn't saying a word. The skin around his eyes was bunched up so tight,
even his lashes seemed swallowed up in it.

Pornographic expletives, inspired with sweet new life,
tried to force their way past my lips, which I pressed together
to avoid freaking Tag out. I leaned down to kiss him but he
sensed my approach. The tickle of my breath along his ear and
cheek must have repelled him. His head jerked away, and now
he was facing straight down. It would have felt good to nose
around in his hair—but I let it go.

Then for the first time that night, my eyes closed. I cried
out, then rolled over to his side.

"Well, that answers a question," he said.

"Don't tell me," I said, trying to catch my breath.

A scratchy scrim of cloud passed across the moon. The crashing waves sounded far away, for the beach was very wide here, this beach that nobody ever used.

Tag jumped up and began gathering his stuff. We made only the most perfunctory efforts to clean up before running back. Stuffed into his tiny car, we seemed bigger than we had been before, or at least to have more limbs.

He started up the engine. "No, I'm not gay. That's what I needed to find out. Thank you."

I had been joking when I told him not to say what I knew he was going to say. In fact I felt a surprising relief. I didn't need him to be gay and his wife certainly didn't need him to be gay and even the homo-deprived Boat Club didn't need him to be gay.

We drove back across the marsh in silence. Tag was staring straight ahead as the oleanders lining the road rushed past. I studied his handsome profile in the underwater glow of the car's interior, knowing I would never get this close to him again.

As we pulled in to the Boat Club parking lot, I thought of my brother. "Hey, Tag," I said.

"Yeah?"

"I didn't notice on the menu, but do they have an appetizer in the restaurant that's oysters two ways or something?"

He turned to me with a smirk. "Oysters two ways, huh. Where'd you hear that?"

I intended to get to the reunion as late as possible, stay for an hour, and leave. Going late would recall the trauma of holding your lunchtray while everyone watched you looking for a place to sit, but at least the evening would be over quickly. And this strategy gave me an excuse to turn Ray down when he asked whether I wanted to go with him and the band.

The main hall—which still served as administrative building, lunchroom, lounge, auditorium, and dance space—had been decorated to look fancy. Silver balloons were strung here and there, and the tables had white tablecloths and flowers and candles. I arrived just after dark, and from the walkway I could see through the glass walls how pretty everything looked. I had the idea that if I left now, it was this warm glow of a memory I could cherish for the rest of my life.

But I went in anyway, because I wasn't going to let Ray have the satisfaction of knowing I was afraid to attend my high school reunion. As I walked through the doorway I heard him singing backup vocals to "Nowhere Man," his voice confirming my feeling that my reunion was all about him. But a woman's voice was singing the melody and she sounded good. There was an unmanned table with a couple of nametags on it, and as I took mine—it would aid in my fantasy of being unrecognizably buff without it—I peered across the dark pit of the dance-floor at the band. The floor was full of bodies that hadn't yet resolved into particular people, and so as I moved along the upper level of the lunchroom, it was easy to ignore the dancers and just head for that voice, sweet and breathy and incongruously coming from a mountain of a girl who, I now saw, was the one from yesterday's karate tournament. She stood behind a microphone and sang, "He's a real nowhere man. . . ." Her short dark hair was slicked back and held in place with a silver barrette.

My brother stood slightly behind her on the bass, and behind him, on the drums, was Ramirez! And on the other side of the singer was the black guy on lead guitar! I took a good look at all the speakers, half expecting to find the infant towhead dancing on one of them, shaking a tambourine. It was strange seeing these people here. For one thing they weren't wearing their pajamalike uniforms. For another, they looked nothing like their audience, who were, as a quick survey confirmed, all white, and dressed like bankers. I stopped moving, staring with wonder at this band of misfits showering light upon this room full of privilege, illuminating nothing less than the dark corners of history itself. Someone handed me a beer, and I caught my brother's attention and for the first time in my life toasted him ungrudgingly. In return he nodded and, I believed, even allowed his lips to curl slightly upward.

"They're good," said a voice in my ear. "Your brother kind of filled out, didn't he?"

It was Tag, looking gorgeous in a dark suit and an open-collared white button-down.

Before thinking better of it I threw my arms around him and he hugged me back.

"I was going to ignore you," I said into his ear.

He let go and frowned. "Why?"

"I don't know, I didn't want it to be weird for you or anything."

"Nothing's ever too weird for me," he said. "Come on, I want you to meet my wife. She's going to wonder where your motorcycle is, in that getup."

Things were getting either stranger or more normal. More normal because this was what I imagined one did at these events—meet the spouses of the people who ignored you in high school. Tag seemed downright giddy at the prospect of this encounter, and I wouldn't have been surprised if he had extended a hand to lead me to it. I nodded goodbye to my brother and followed Tag through the darkness to one of the candlelit tables.

"This is my sugarpie," he said, kissing a small dark woman on top of her head.

"Hi, I'm Susan," she said, extending a hand.

"My Jewish sugarpie." He kissed her on the cheek. "Isn't she beautiful?"

She was pretty but not of the leggy blond cheerleader variety he had once favored. She looked me in the eye. She was from Atlanta, which practically counted as the North down here, and she seemed like someone I might be friends with in New York. I appreciated how suspiciously she was eyeing me.

Tag sat with us for a couple of minutes, but he kept jumping up to say hello to people, at one point whispering in the ear of a person I believed to be Cathy Perkins, his high school girlfriend. She had gotten heavy.

"Okay, y'all," he finally said, putting down his empty beer bottle and standing up. "I'll be right back. Dance with my wife, will you, Edward? I'm sure you know how to dance by now."

Susan didn't seem to mind or even notice Tag's fidgetiness and sudden disappearance.

"You didn't know how to dance in high school?" she asked, trying to decode her husband's last remark. "You've taken classes since then?"

"I'm gay." I made little disco gestures with my hands. "That's what he meant. You know, Studio 54, gay bars, and all that?"

She laughed reluctantly.

"I've heard it before," I said.

"You know, I'm trying to think if he's ever mentioned your name."

"I doubt it. We weren't really that close."

She looked perplexed but I had no explanation to give her.

"So you're an architect?" I asked.

"I am."

"Tag too? I just assumed—"

She laughed more freely now. "No, Winson's the one who

goes out and gets the clients. It's so sunny here, but it would never occur to anyone to put up solar panels if my husband didn't badger them about it at the Club."

"He's good at charming people."

"He tells me he took you there last night," she said.

A sick feeling spewed in my stomach. But why shouldn't he have told her he took me to the Club? What was wrong with that?

"He did. He thought I would want to join."

She seemed to find this hilarious. "Did he tell you about the challah?"

"Yes," I said, more easily. "And the lobsters."

"That's one of the great things about Winson. He has no idea why that's funny."

There was, apparently, a reunion going on around us. Some people were dancing, others were sitting at tables talking and drinking. Was food coming? Had people already eaten? Was there going to be some kind of speech? What I really wanted was to listen to my brother's band, whose name, I realized, I didn't even know. I was a terrible brother, absolutely the worst. I refilled Susan's glass and my own. Besides the music and the fact that Ollie Byrd wasn't in my class, the one undeniably nice thing about this reunion was the bottle of Maker's Mark on each table.

"Should we dance?" I asked.

"Why not?" she replied.

Now the band was playing "Rolling on the River." The big girl wasn't trying to be Tina Turner, but her version was spicier than the Creedence Clearwater Revival version they were still playing on the radio down here. Ray was taking it pretty fast, thereby sparing me the awkwardness of slow-dancing with Tag's wife. We were moving about, a little randomly but not without animation. Nobody cut in, but every now and then someone would touch me on the back or say something in my ear. I was vague about who some of these people were and I couldn't hear a word of what they were saying. It was a partial but not unpleasant experience of the world, like being in a dream.

And then a rumbling went through the crowd, heads turned, and there, emerging from the shadows to the right of the stage, were Cathy Perkins and Donna Showalter, wearing their Peter Pan blouses and checked cheerleading skirts. Donna wasn't as fat as Cathy, but these were still two large women and in their uniforms they looked, well, awful. I had always thought their confidence came from their looks, but I was wrong. The friends they had grown up with started to clap and my brother cued the band to stop. It didn't seem as though anyone had let him in on this.

Halfway down the length of the pit, still on the upper level, the women came to a stop and turned to face us.

"Be aggressive!" they shouted, shaking pompoms they pulled from behind their backs. Someone turned on the lights. "Be all aggressive! Y'all, be aggressive, be all aggressive! Y'all, be aggressive, be all aggressive!"

They weren't doing splits but they were bending and high-kicking in a game approximation of their old moves, and everyone hooted appreciatively.

Then they shook their pompoms in the direction of the music room, where out of the shadows emerged Tag, bare-legged, in his famous wraparound skirt and espadrilles.

"Be aggressive!" the women shouted. "Be all aggressive!"

But they were the only ones making a sound. The crowd was staring at Tag. He was wearing the same blouse as the women, but he'd tied it into a knot at the bottom, exposing his soft belly, going for, I guess, a trailer park kind of look. The legs themselves were thicker, and thickness was the overall impression he gave. That and vanished youth.

Was this funny? Did anyone want to see this husband and father do this? Tag, my beautiful Tag, what have you done now?

I turned to Susan with an apologetic look but she just shrugged.

Now he was moving, throwing his arms over his head and kicking wildly. He jumped, fell to his knees, and jumped again. He spun around and shook his ass. Someone had to save him from the silence of the room, and suddenly there came the terrible knowledge that it was going to be me. In high school I had succeeded at making myself invisible, most importantly here, in the lunchroom. Now I started clapping and stared straight ahead as everyone looked my way. An aeon passed before Susan joined me, and then someone else. "Tag!" a voice called out, and finally the room broke into laughter and applause.

Our classmates' delayed but genuine enthusiasm encouraged Tag to make an effort at a split that was hilarious in its failure. Maybe it was because he was more established in the world, maybe it was because he had gotten fucked on a sand dune the night before—whatever the reason, he was going at it with an even greater sense of liberation than he had shown in high school. No gay person acted this way, no drag queen knew these moves. Only a safely married ladies' man like Tag could get away with a performance like this.

But when I looked over at my brother I could see these nuances were lost on him. Within the narrow range of emotion his face allowed, he seemed amazed at the level of faggishness on display here in the lunchroom. I waited for the usual feeling to start inside me, the tightening up, the closing off of sympathy. But it didn't come, and instead I just smiled at him, my brother, for I shared his amazement, and when I turned back to Tag I even let myself laugh a little.

"Give it up for Tag Kingsley," Ray announced, while Ramirez did something on the drums.

Everyone applauded.

"Tag Kingsley," my brother said again, his lips right up against the microphone. He wasn't smiling, of course, but a look of faint amusement appeared on his face and I wondered where this was heading. At one point he had introduced the members of the band but otherwise he hadn't said anything until now. He had been content to do what he had done as a kid, watch silently, blackly.

But he had, apparently, also been thinking. Some plot was taking shape. "Hey, great legs, Tag," he said.

I stood there wincing.

"Ahooooooooo, werewolf of London," Ray sang, accompanying himself on bass.

And now I could see people turning to one another with a smile, a terrible one, nothing like the way they had been smiling at Tag. They had been laughing with Tag but now they were starting to laugh at my brother.

"She's got legs," Ray sang. "She knows how to use them."

He was miscalculating. Of course, I had too. Basking in the band's glow, I identified with them precisely because they were outsiders. But Ray believed he had become an insider. What else was this patter, these song quotes, but the same kind of crap he spewed at the gym and the sports bar? This was why he was so comfortable doing his lame roast of Tag Kingsley, who was, yes, making a fool of himself but who Ray didn't seem to realize was still one of them.

I pushed my way toward the stage.

"Give it up for Tag Kingsley," my brother said. "Or is that his sister, Tag Queensley?"

No one laughed. All Ray had to do was launch into a song, something untopical and fun, like "China Grove," a song he could do in his sleep. Everyone would forget about the grotesque little pep rally and start dancing again. My brother would be saved. I just had to make a request.

But I didn't get there fast enough.

"She was a gay stripper," he sang. "Gay stripper, yeah. It took me soooooooo long to find out."

It was rushing through me, pumping up out of me, all the feeling I had never been able to summon for Ray. Unnatural brother no more! Now I was at the front of the pit, a step below the stage. I jumped up and threw my arms around him in one movement. I held on to his waist and he stumbled backward, right into the drums.

He got up and I caught him again, this time around his upper body. He felt so solid and strong. He freed his arms and I felt a hot quick jab to my neck. All the air in my body seemed to fly out of my mouth and I staggered backward, expecting any second to fall into the pit. He grabbed my shirt collar and yanked me toward him, either to save me from breaking my neck or to take advantage of my stumble.

I was tired of this kind of ambiguity in our relationship.

I knocked away his hands and righted myself. He tried to punch me in the stomach but I twisted out of the way. He had lost his footing and I managed to lock my arms around his head. I was bigger than he was, I could wrestle him down to the stage.

It was his athlete-at-peak-performance look, that's what I saw in Ray's eyes, and suddenly I was scared of him. How far would he go? No referee was going to cite illegal moves, neither his nor mine. No one seemed to be coming to break us apart. My brother tried to pry me off but I didn't dare let go. He pivoted and kicked me behind my knee—he was going for every soft spot I had—and my legs buckled. But I kept my arms wrapped tightly around him.

All the World's a Field

They were moving and the cow wasn't coming with them.

Miriam's son Shmuel referred to the cow in Yiddish, though he and his brother had stopped speaking and understanding the language two and a half years ago. That had been at Chanukah. Miriam had pointed out to Izzy, her oldest grandson, that the wagon he had just freed from its box, a present from her, looked so much like the wagons loaded with hay that used to pass through her village in the summer. She was speaking to her grandson, not to her sons, but they both turned to her and glared. It had been a plan, prearranged. "From now on we don't speak Yiddish in this house," Shmuel, who called himself Sam, said. "I know you understand what we're saying, you've lived here long enough," his brother, Moishe, who called himself Moe, chimed in. He lived next door. "My kids grow up speaking English exclusively, is that understood?" Shmuel said. Moishe nodded, seconding his brother. The wives regarded her from slyly lowered lids, their mouths two lines. Izzy played with his wagon. He didn't care what language was spoken in the house, as long as it came from the heart. Miriam leaned over and mussed his hair. "Shainkeit," she said,

47

stroking the golden down on his head. Beauty. Shmuel pointed a finger at her heart and said, "I mean it."

And so he had. At first when Miriam spoke to him in Yiddish Shmuel answered in English. Then he just made a face at her. Then he stopped turning his head, refusing to acknowledge that she was speaking, making sound, opening her mouth. That she was even there. Yet the punishment of being ignored she had not found so punishing. The inevitable threat to keep her from the grandchildren had not materialized, because, after all, she lived in the same house as two of them and next door to the other three. Also, no one could deny she had eventually complied—she no longer spoke Yiddish to the grandchildren or to anyone else in the house. Nor did she speak any other language—she had not learned English and did not intend to, though she understood everything she needed to understand. She understood all too well. Shmuel thought she was angry, but she was not. She lived in a peaceful silence with her memories of Nur and her cow.

She believed Shmuel held against her the failure of his strategy. And because it was his fault, his failure, she knew he would never forgive her. She had had a husband once, a shoemaker but a scholar at heart. How proud she had been of him, how happy lying in his arms as the words tumbled from his racing brain. The rabbi led a study group *Shabbes* afternoons, and when Tsvi came home he filled her with questions, ostensibly of a legal nature but truly little stories. "If I find two coins stacked by the side of the road, are they mine?" he once asked her, and she could see her Tsvi coming down some country lane with that rich man's swagger of his, the faraway look in his blue eyes, the shine on his golden ear curls. He asked this question and actually waited to hear what she would say. As always she had to come up with something, some nonsensical guess, before he would reveal the answer, which led always to another question. What she learned from all this, besides the excellence of her husband, was that not only every word but also every letter counted—this, as far as she could tell, was what all the Bible verses and commentaries boiled down to. And now her son Shmuel, who had not taken so much after his father, was paying the price for his carelessness. He had issued his tsar's edict that Yiddish not be spoken in the house, he had conscripted his children into the American language, but at no point did he decree she speak English herself. Perhaps he had assumed she would.

Miriam believed he would no longer recognize his own mother's voice in the unlikely event she should find it again.

She was certainly in no danger of forgetting her son's voice. *We're moving and the* behayma *isn't coming with us. Behayma*— the beast, also said of people, incomprehensibly, as if comparing someone to an animal meant the person was stupid. Her son, avowed enemy of Yiddish, had said to her one word in Yiddish. When he wanted her to understand, this was the language that came out.

And in what language was she permitted to deliver her response?

Redness spread like a tide across Shmuel's face. He hitched his thumbs into his pants.

"Well?" he asked.

Madwoman, mute, Miriam moved between the rows of wooden bungalows in the bluing light. Her pail swung from one arm and her little stool from the other. The ground was sandy beneath her feet—there were no paving stones here, or grass, just acorns and burrs and a swordlike weed, and fat roots bubbling out of the ground. It was an exciting and paradoxical time of day. As things in the world resolved, gaining authority, they also seemed to lose it. They broke apart. They shifted from place to place. Clotheslines, jutting palmetto frond, tricycle overturned in the sand, unidentifiable thing by the side of a house—look again and they were not where they had been. Chickens peered out at her from their coops, softly clucking, like the engine of the world warming up. Gulls whistled, and from the main road two blocks away the deliverymen were heard making their rounds.

The houses ended at a fenced-in lot with a few patches of grass. It was light enough to see the cow looking in her direction, as it always did. She would not say the cow was smiling but obviously it was happy to see her. Its dark liquid eyes did not project the melancholy look of cows at all. You could sense its anticipation. It had intelligence. Of course it knew what she had come to do—but there was something more. Occasionally its ears flicked forward like the stroke of a paddle, it took a step to find fresh grass, but otherwise it did not move and in its solidity and stillness it projected a definite self-consciousness. It knew her, it knew itself. It was a black cow with a white belly, and as the light went from blue to gray to yellow, as the world took on a scratchy appearance, ready to snap into itself or dissolve, the cow seemed to stand apart, unchanging. It existed in a realm out of time and place, and she remembered Tsvi talking this way about God.

She sat and stroked the cow's bristly hair, she pressed her nose into its side and smelled its warm sweetness. Her family believed she had an unhealthy attachment to this beast. This was not true. She alone in the family had a country girl's attitude toward animals. She cut chickens' throats, singed off their pinfeathers. She koshered meat, rubbing it with salt and patiently watching the blood drip into the pan as the children ran screaming out of the kitchen and her daughter-in-law looked on with distaste. Her sons were away at the shoeshop during the day, they never witnessed this supposed carnage, and perhaps when their wives told them in bed of her old-world savagery (which incidentally had enabled them to eat their dinner), her boys did not recall that they had witnessed the same things when they were growing up, before she had sent them with their uncle to America.

She could have been a slaughterer. And even with this cow she limited her affections. When she was fresh off the boat, when she was still a novelty in America and her family indulged her, they happily complied with her desire for a cow. Actually, they had to do nothing at all except reap the profits—the wonderful fresh milk on the table, the extra money from her delivery rounds. She had not even expected them to help her procure the cow. She could see right away that here in Savannah, Georgia, her sons had become city people. And so she had Mr. Shankman from the Workman's Circle take her out to the country.

She chose this one immediately, she felt a certain connection—and yet she did not name it or even think of it as a *she* most of the time. In Nur Miriam was friends with a peasant girl whose family kept pigs. She only named the runt of each litter, and this piglet she would make her pet, nursing it with a bottle, fattening it up, but not shedding a tear when the time came for it to be killed. Miriam had found this behavior cold but somehow admirable. She herself did not think she would be able to part so easily with an animal she had named.

The cow, impatient, stamped its front legs. Miriam laughed. The cow whimpered. She laughed again and set to work. She hadn't named her cow and so parting with it would not be so hard. But she did not intend to part with it. Where they were moving was a mystery—there was an outing scheduled this weekend to see the house—but surely something could be arranged. Mainly on their wives' urging, she felt, her sons were not happy living in this neighborhood of poor Jews,

Yiddish squawkers every one of them. But Miriam herself did not find the situation ideal. She had to walk ten minutes to see her cow, who for its part had to stand in its humble lot lonely and unwatched most of the day.

"It's a wonderful house," said Shmuel's wife, Dora, washing something at the sink. "It's a double house, really, with white columns in front in the plantation style. You are going to love it when you see it."

The goose in Miriam's lap had stopped struggling. It was swaddled in her apron and with her left hand Miriam held open its beak. There was a bowl of mashed corn on the table and Miriam dropped a bit into the goose's mouth, then pushed the paste down. Other women used some kind of object, a spoon maybe, but Miriam would not do something like this to a poor bird, in such an awkward position to begin with. Wrapped in a bit of *shmatte*, her finger plunged again and again. Under such circumstances the goose could not quite manage to bite. Miriam was quick—in two seconds the corn was gone and the goose ready for more.

Her grandsons peeked in from the doorway, pretending they were not there, but nevertheless responding to Miriam's beckoning finger, wrapped in its dirty rag, by shaking their heads.

"You'll see it on Sunday," Dora was saying. "It's so big there's a room for you on both sides."

So this had something to do with it—back and forth between the half houses she would bounce like a ball.

"The finer families are all moving out there." Dora brought a dripping colander of green beans to the table and began stringing them onto newspaper. "The Gutentags just bought a house on the same block. We ourselves have always brought up the children to treat everyone alike, but it's what they hear at school—"

Miriam looked at her and nodded.

"And more than once the other kids have taunted my children," Dora went on. "You must admit there are colored families living not two blocks away."

So now Miriam understood. But look! There was Izzy sneaking across the kitchen. Miriam looked down at the goose and tried not to smile. Dora turned in his direction and said, "Honey, go out and play."

He froze, hoping this would restore his invisibility, but Dora did not turn away. She pointed a bean at him. "I don't want you touching that nasty goose."

That they were going to eat and enjoy one day very soon, Miriam would have liked to explain to her grandson. But she sensed he understood.

Now Izzy was standing alongside Dora. His younger brother, Ike, seemed to have taken a step or two into the room.

"I want to feed the bird," Izzy said bravely.

"This is your grandmother's job," Dora said, frowning. "Your father has a weakness for goose."

Miriam smiled at Izzy, the terror leaching from his face.

"I don't know why you encourage him," Dora said. "Oh, I guess it's not your fault," she quickly put in, and Miriam wondered how she could have possibly given the impression of being offended by anything her silly daughter-in-law had said.

"This is why Sam and I decided to move, and Moe and Evelyn agree. Everyone has a menagerie around here," Dora continued. "It's just the way people live. I don't think it's a healthful environment for children at all."

Izzy held a bit of corn between two fingers.

"Just be careful," Dora said.

Miriam pried the goose's beak open and nodded to Izzy to go. He looked straight down its throat and dropped in the corn. Miriam laughed. He flinched but stood his ground. He looked down at his fingers, and when he saw they were still there he reached into the bowl and said, "Another."

"All right, one more," Dora said, "then I want you and your brother"—who was on the advance—"to go out and play."

The goose kicked and first Izzy and then little Ike screamed and fled from the kitchen. Miriam pressed down what was in the goose's mouth and pushed aside the bowl, which was almost empty anyway. She wrapped both arms around the hot goose in her lap and smiled sympathetically at her daughter-in-law, who turned away. Dora looked hard at the grecn bean in her hand and tore off the string.

With the life she had lived Miriam thought she was prepared for anything, but as the motorcar approached the house she saw she was wrong. In the infernal machine they had moved bumpily through the city, past the grand rowhouses on their brick and cobblestone streets downtown, through the beautiful squares, one after another. South, south, past the park, past the end of the trolley tracks, where who knew anyone even lived. But the pine-forest had been cut away here and the streets had numbers and not names, and as they turned down Thirty-seventh Street she recognized the house from Dora's description. It was a great yellow wooden house with four fluted white columns supported on square bases; there was a wide porch with a balustrade and two screened front doors right next to each other. But the house disappeared from her awareness when the car stopped and a green field in back was revealed. This was a cow pasture, bigger than the lot in which her cow currently lived, and she felt as if a knife had been plunged into her heart.

This house was not in the plantation style, it was a plantation. Miriam had never seen one but she knew. She turned to Dora, who would not look at her—and Miriam understood why. A herd of cows could live back here. She squeezed her eyes shut—she saw her Tsvi and for one terrible instant longed for the day when she would meet him in death.

Shmuel helped her down. He and his wife and his brother and his wife and all their children ran joyfully onto the property. The children slid along the railing of the porch. The men stood on the curb with a proprietary air and exchanged a few words. The women, their skirts hemmed above their ankles, paused in the shade to admire the azalea bushes, which were at the height of their beauty, loaded with pink and white blooms. Miriam stood in a patch of dirt. She walked over to the front steps and sat, facing the street, where she could not see the yard. A horse-drawn carriage passed, then another, and the moss bearding the oaks on either side of the street swayed in the breeze.

"Let's all go see the yard and then we can go inside," Shmuel called out, and Moishe seconded this, as was his way. "Come on, Ma," Shmuel said and Miriam indicated they should go on ahead.

"You don't want to see the yard?" Shmuel asked.

Miriam shook her head.

"All right, don't see it." Shmuel sat down alongside her. Moishe caught his brother's eye and Shmuel said, "Go on, we'll catch up."

And so here they were, mother and son, Jews, sitting on the steps of a plantation house. Somewhere. She had not left a trail of breadcrumbs; if they left her here alone, she would never be able to find her way back home.

"It's a beautiful house, isn't it?" he tried.

She shrugged.

He stopped trying. "I thought you'd be proud of me."

And she was, of course she was.

"You don't really think we're going to bring a cow out here, do you?"

He seemed to have made up his mind.

"I don't know what you want that cow for anyway." He scratched one side of his head and then the other—a nervous habit. "How many customers do you have left anyway, two? People have milk delivered from the dairy now, a milkman in a cap, not a lady with a cow. It's 1927, Ma, not the Dark Ages." He leaned backward and gestured to the magnificence of the house. "Does this look like you need to work like a peasant woman?"

Goodbye to the cow—he had made this point again and again. Who was he trying to convince?

He took out his handkerchief and wiped his forehead, though it was not so hot—the murderous heat was, if they were lucky, still another month away.

"If you still had that kid to help you out, that would be one thing," Shmuel said. "But even he could see the way the wind was blowing."

It was true she had had a helper once, to keep the lot clean and shelter the cow in winter—then one day he was gone.

"You aren't in Nur anymore," her son pointed out. "Though frankly you act like you are. Moe agrees with me on this and he doesn't think it's too healthy. And why you'd want to pretend you were living in a shtetl full of Jew-haters who killed your own husband—"

He was angry at his father's death, though why he should take it out on her she didn't understand.

"And don't look at me that way, Ma. I am not going to feel guilty for giving you the life of a queen in the greatest country on earth. Just because I don't want my children growing up socialists with a cow in their backyard, this is not something to be ashamed of!"

The children had been pulled out of the Workman's Circle School, where Yiddish was taught but not Hebrew, after her insecure daughters-in-law overheard someone in a store saying it was a school for godless low-class socialists and then laughing, obviously at them.

"Daddy!" Little Izzy appeared and Shmuel opened his arms. "Come play in the backyard with us."

Shmuel turned to his mother triumphantly, then lifted his son over his head and went down the steps.

Ever since she was told they were moving she had been thinking vaguely about what arrangements she could make with her cow. Some houses in their current neighborhood had yards, which would have been ideal. Even if the yard was modest, she was sure her sons would eventually see the benefits of keeping the cow there, despite their stated hostility to the idea. They were doing well in their business, but she did not think they were rich enough to move into the downtown, where some of the German Jews had moved in alongside the descendants of generations of Savannah gentiles. Still, she considered this possibility as well. The walled gardens, the narrow lanes—a cow would not have been happy in the downtown and this she might have been able to accept. But there, on that Thirty-seventh Street plantation, there!

In Nur her family had once sold a calf, and its mother would not stop crying. It was unbearable—they finally had to sell the mother too. Miriam's cow, in its humble and quiet way, was making its own demands. It was producing less and less milk, as if to alert her to the poorness of its lot. Maybe it knew she had so few customers. If questioned her cow could be no more wrong than her son—she still had three customers, not two, as Shmuel had tauntingly claimed. She did not know how she would get her cow to its new home, but she knew this was where it belonged.

And so the first order of business was to let her customers know she would no longer be able to make deliveries. Perhaps in the wilderness to which her sons were moving there were people who wanted fresh milk. All she knew was that it would be impossible to schlep bottles to the old neighborhood, where all three customers lived. It would be hard on them. She would let them know today so they could make other arrangements.

Her silence had lasted so long that speaking was no longer an option. Not-speaking had become a medium to her, like water to a fish; emerging into the upperworld of speech seemed like death. But there was no need to speak. With her sons she needed only to tilt her head or scratch an itch—no, she needed to do nothing at all to hear a response she did not want to hear. Accusations and recriminations, denials and threats—it saddened her that life weighed so heavily on Shmuel's heart that a blink of an eye from his own mother could release all this. Life did not weigh so heavily on Miriam; her transactions in the world were pleasant and smooth. You do not need to speak to have your chicken plucked; you hand it to the woman whose job it is to do this all day long. You smile, you nod, you shake your head. You point to a fish, lift a bunch of greens off the pile. They knew her in City Market. The merchants who weren't Jewish never had heard her say much more than hello or good day. If they were Jewish, they seemed to understand when she no longer spoke Yiddish; they had a lot of silences in their own lives as well, forgetting was general in America, a condition of existence. And there was this truth: people liked to talk, and once they found someone to wordlessly listen, they didn't complain!

As for her customers, she saw them around the neighborhood, but as their milkmaid she never saw them at all and so had no occasion to speak. She swooped down upon their stoops at dawn. She left them their bottles of milk with the wonderful yellowish cream on top, sealed tightly against waiting birds and squirrels. Then into the half-light she hurried away.

She did not speak and could not write, not even in Yiddish. She sat in the kitchen and considered her dilemma. Dora was out with the children. Miriam drank her tea and looked at the newspaper. She liked the drawings of elegant elongated women. Today half a page was taken up with a single advertisement. There was writing at the top and bottom, but in the middle was a very realistic drawing of the storefront of Cohen's Fine Millinery and Apparel. It was a shame, he had been put out of business by another Jew, Abe Tenenbaum, whose emporium kept adding and expanding departments, a very modern Ladies Hats being the latest. When Miriam passed Meyer Cohen's shop in its last days and seen the bargain-hunters hunched like vultures over the bins, she realized with some guilt that the hat on her head came from Tenenbaum's. Meyer had closed his doors yesterday. This was no advertisement for a sale. From the days when Dora used to read the paper to her, she knew what it was.

She found a drawing of a smiling and garlanded cow's head on the very next page.

When Shankman looked up from his desk it was with such a smile that Miriam's insides flooded with warmth. "Miriam, maideleh, zit zit!" he said, rising and moving his own cushioned metal chair from behind the desk and taking a plain wooden chair for himself.

She laughed at this gallantry, at an old lady being called a little girl. They sat next to each other and smiled into each other's eyes. She had not seen him in a long time. Shankman looked even younger than before. His face had a healthy ruddy color and his scalp glowed. But there were tufts of dirty hair growing out of his ears that made her feel such a tenderness toward him. She wished his wife would do something about those ears—they were in her hands now, without hair on his head he apparently no longer saw a barber.

They were sitting in his office at the Workman's Circle. She was never entirely certain what he did there, though she was sure he still went to greet the trains and boats. He loved doing this. God had obviously called him for this purpose. He had been there when her boat came in. He came up and introduced himself before she could even find her sons. He was from a village in Poland not far from Nur. How fortunate for her that her first conversation in America was with this kind man! She sat now and listened to him speak. He did not expect her to reply. He understood, and she wondered if he felt some continuing responsibility for the Jews he greeted, if he felt some responsibility for her.

She listened to what he said and did not say. Did he indulge her because he thought she was mad? Yes, of course—but madness is a vast country, its topography so varied, its states so unalike. Did he think she had forgotten how to speak because she had been unsuccessful at forgetting the other thing? Her husband, along with every other member of the rabbi's study group, dragged through the streets—but this is not what killed him, at least not directly. He had lived for two more years, during which time they sent the children away and planned their own escape—his spirit had not been broken, he pictured the future, and this was not death but life. He had died suddenly in his sleep, in her arms, who knew of what? She knew only that he had not died one second before the last breath left his body—every second of his life he had lived! She would have liked to tell Shankman this. She would have liked to tell him she hardly thought about this thing her bitter sons must constantly have thought about, the memory of which they had devoted their lives to erasing. She thought a hundred times more of the taste of her husband's thick golden-furred forearm as she ran her tongue up and down it.

Miriam reached into her bag and retrieved two things: a pint of freshly made sour cream and her notice. With flour paste she had glued the cow's head over the picture of the store. She had managed only to get two other copies of the newspaper and so she could not let Shankman have this, but it was good enough, he would be able to see.

He stuck a finger into the sour cream and plunged it into his mouth, his eyes narrowing in rapture. "Batamt!" he exclaimed. Delicious. Then he looked at the clipping and asked, "What's this?" He read aloud in English: "'To our valued customers. The pleasure has been ours serving you for 24 years. Alas, all good things must come to an end and now we must close our doors. We thank each and every one of you from the bottom of our hearts.' Then what's this here, a picture of a cow?"

He laughed but Miriam could see the concern in his eyes. She laughed too, to show she found her handicraft funny.

He looked her in the eye, expecting something. If he had been a customer of hers, he would have understood. She pointed to the sour cream and then the cow, and she pressed a hand to her heart.

"Ah, your beautiful black cow, I remember her," he said. "How is she doing?"

She shrugged.

Then a look of understanding. "They tell me you're moving."

She nodded. He knew everything that went on in the Jewish community, he would be able to fix anything.

"To a fancy place practically in the country," he continued. "*Kein ahora*, those boys of yours must be doing all right."

She looked longingly at the drawing of the cow, which did not completely cover the drawing of the hat shop. A cow's head, decorated, prepared maybe for some pagan sacrifice, appeared to have been left in the middle of a street.

"You want me to look after your cow?"

No, no, she wouldn't presume such a thing.

"You're selling her?"

She shook her head.

"So who is going to look after your cow?"

She pointed to herself.

"Aha, you need to move your cow!" he exclaimed.

She didn't understand why more people didn't conserve their breath by going the route of silence.

Die ganster veldt ist ein feldt. All the world's a field—this was what Tsvi had said when reassuring her their children would be safe in America, that they would thrive there. Miriam rolled her eyes. A silly old expression repeated so often that it barely meant anything anymore—how could this possibly have helped a woman about to send her own children away? She interrogated him. Would they have Jew-haters in America like Nur? she asked. Undoubtedly! he merrily replied. And so why were they doing this? she demanded. Because, he said, they have something in America that they don't have here, and that's hope. And so what did his expression mean? Would America look like Nur? He laughed and said parts of it probably did. He said they and their children and grandchildren would walk through forests and pick flowers in fields and sit on the banks of a river in the shadow of a mill, and it would all be familiar, even to the little ones who had never been to Nur, familiar but also brand-new. They would keep goats and chickens and meditate on Torah near the stillness of cows, and they would feel God's presence wherever they went.

And so in Tsvi's mouth the old words had been given new life.

Miriam was on her way now to see her cow. She had come straight from Shankman's office. The sun shone through the pines; the birds sang and her heart sang too. Shankman would arrange things and he would do it fast—they were moving in a week's time. If Shankman did feel some responsibility for her, for her success in the new world, she hoped he felt no responsibility for her craziness. He was a good man, a mensch, and she was indebted to him for everything that had gone right here. So much of it had. And once they got the cow to the plantation, there would be some tsuris, some trouble, at first, but eventually the cow would become part of the landscape, as cows do.

The sandy path ended at the last little house, and there in the lot she saw her cow was gone. Then into the silence of the sky rose the first sound that had come out of her mouth since anyone could remember. Memory was short and silence was long, but apparently it did not last forever. Her wordless cry filled the empty spaces of the world. People emerged from their houses to witness the spectacle of a mute madwoman raging at nothing. But they kept their distance. Mothers clutched their children's hands, dogs whined.

Miriam shook her fist at the sky, at her fool of a husband, who had obviously known nothing about America. Round and round she went, blue spots and red spots danced before her eyes in the glare—and now someone was coming from between the houses. It was Shmuel, someone must have sent for him. He seized her by the arms and held her until she stopped moving, though her head still spun. She could smell his breath, see the sweat glistening in the big pores of his nose. She gulped down the hot humid air and coughed it right back up.

"You won't talk," he said. "It would have been no use trying to have a conversation with you."

"Slaughterer!" she cried, struggling out of his grip and slapping his cheek.

His mouth dropped open. "You speak English."

"Butcher!"

"Ma," he said, holding up his hands.

"Thief!"

"It was Dora's idea," he said weakly, his eyes filling with tears. "We had to do something, we're moving next week."

Of course her daughter-in-law didn't want her kids growing up around a cow, a goose, chickens . . . she didn't want them growing up around a crazy old woman, a mute, a newspaper cutter, a slaughterer at heart! Her son the slaughterer was only taking after her.

"I am in a terrible position!" he cried.

"My cow, what you do with it?" she demanded.

"My God, you speak English," he said, shaking his head.

Apparently, this was something he couldn't get past. But Miriam had had much greater surprises in her life of late. Why should anything surprise her in a world so in need of repair that a hundred times a day she saw opportunities to fix it?

"Where is my cow!"

"We sold it back to the farm where you bought it," he said, dry-eyed and quiet. "They came today and took it away."

She had been wrong about so many things. Her son still recognized her voice, even speaking a foreign tongue. She was breathing softly now. She released herself from his grip and sank into the dirt, hugging her skirts against her ankles. Sand gnats flew at her face and she brushed them away. Her neighbors' eyes were on her but she started to feel quite calm.

Sitting in her son's shadow, she looked up. "Your papa did not want this."

She had not meant to say this, it just came out, and now it was she holding up her hands to ward off a blow. She had remembered too late—there were risks involved in speaking. Shmuel was always angry, he could not talk about his father without screaming at her. And so when the blow did not come she prepared herself, as best she could, for the lashes she would receive from her son's tongue. She put down her hands and waited.

The Cantor's Miracles

I

The window glowed like a funhouse. Fluorescent tubes placed out of sight illuminated a jumble of tchotchkes on narrow glass shelves. The display was mostly crystal and colored glass, shaped into useful objects like vases and bowls and useless ones like kittens and elves and Uga the university mascot, backed by a mirror in which the cantor could see himself thinking the obvious, that this was a window that invited you to smash it in. At that hour the main street was desolate, darkness stretched between puddles of light under the buzzing streetlamps. And yet this window had light to spare, it flooded you with brightness, filling in wrinkles, obscuring by bedazzling. The cantor had to admit he looked wonderful. With his hat tilted at a rakish angle he seemed charming and prosperous, and no one would know the suffering in his heart. What was in this window was dreck, but it was expensive and the cantor couldn't have touched it if he wanted to. Worse, the things in the window reminded you of what they ostentatiously omitted, the good stuff inside, the diamonds and silver and gold that Siegel didn't dare put out for public view.

The cantor didn't look in this window much. But he lived in an apartment house downtown, on the shadowy edges of the historic district, and sometimes at night, when he couldn't sleep, he risked being mugged walking the few blocks here to stare. He never came back during the day, he never went inside—there was no point to this. But window-shopping was free, and the cantor got something out of it that he didn't understand. The urge to smash in the window wasn't an angry one, it was more of an impulsion, a force, and impersonal, the way water rushing to find its level says nothing about the water. It was like the filling of a void, a law of nature, and how different really were the forces of destruction from those of creation? The cantor, like any other man, could be but the vessel for these forces, both of which, after all, were divine. As for the cantor himself, it certainly wasn't to use a mirror that he came here. Though he could see himself quite well, he much preferred looking into the window slantwise, from just the right angle to see these treasures, objects of someone else's desire, stretch into the backworld of the mirror in an infinity of repetitions. He was reminded of the Ark of the Covenant, with its covers and curtains and veils, its mysteries of time and space.

Whether the window allayed his suffering or increased it, the cantor suffered from his poverty.

He had been the cantor of a shul in downtown Baltimore whose congregation got smaller and smaller over the years he was there. It would have vanished into nothing anyway, not having the money to build a big new sanctuary out past the ring road where all the Jews were moving. The cantor did nothing more than abandon a sinking ship, an escape hastened by a flirtation he'd had with a married lady. Nothing had happened— but rumors have a life of their own, and he was the victim of this particular one. He took what he could get, as fast as he could, for he also had alimony to pay to a demon of an ex-wife.

What he got was a position as cantor at a Conservative shul in Savannah, Georgia, with a decent-sized congregation that wasn't going anywhere, having already fled the city's core. The brand-new synagogue was on the suburban south side and looked vaguely like a pagoda; it had a certain flair. But his office was small, and off the junior congregation room. The rabbi's office was large, and off the main sanctuary. Certain things couldn't be helped; rabbis were more important than cantors. Still, the contract the cantor signed stunk.

Whereas the congregation provided a house within walking distance for the rabbi to live in, rent free, the cantor had no such perks. His salary placed him above the poverty line, but just barely. He was paid like a waiter, the management expecting him to hustle for tips. And so like a schnorrer he relied on gifts the parents gave him when he had finished preparing their children for their bar mitzvah ceremonies—but unlike a beggar he wasn't allowed to ask. Sometimes the parents forgot or didn't know to begin with. Sometimes they tipped him what they would leave a hotel maid for a single night's stay—and he had worked with their sons and daughters for months. It was the parents who were tipping him, though the money always was handed over by the bar or bat mitzvah—strange ritual that wasn't on the shul's Hebrew school curriculum. The cantor would have liked to suggest, respectfully, that the child actually furnish the money himself. The haul from the big event was always significant—the children talked about it openly, most of them seeming to regard his singing lessons as a financial investment—and so perhaps a certain percentage should be accorded him, perhaps as minimal as ten percent, a tithe as in the days of old.

But he never made this suggestion. The cantor gave the parents their money's worth. He polished his shoes until he could see his reflection in them—but other than the white rubber ones he wore on the High Holidays, they were his only pair. The jewels in his rings were fake. His ties only looked like silk, and the matching pocket squares were in fact bunched bits of nylon stapled to the top of cardboard rectangles imprinted with the name and address of his dry cleaner. As for his always-gleaming teeth, he had had his own pulled and these made at the medical college in Augusta, by a student trying for his license. The procedure was more or less supervised, the boy passed; but they weren't a good fit.

The cantor had a girlfriend, a Leah Bodziner who came from a village in the district adjoining his own, though naturally they didn't know each other over there. Now she worked in a location convenient to his, on the other side of the lobby, down a short hall. She was a Hebrew teacher, a widow, a survivor like himself. Her hair was red. Her mode was scorn. The endless number of know-nothings they brought before her did not depress her. Her scorn for these children energized her, it kept her alive. She used it in her teaching and sometimes managed to get through to them, and on those occasions she was happy to see that her scorn was not justified and her efforts not in vain.

She had grown up in a district famous for its lakes—the cantor, whose own village had nothing distinguished about it, brought up the lakes the first time they met. Lakes! she said. From the time she was a child she had worked with her mother in the market, she had had no time for lakes—she could tell him about pogroms and about mud so deep it could break a wagon wheel, if he was interested. He had never been to the lakes either. But now, when they were together, they went. Their conversations were conducted in three languages, but they went to the lakes in silence. In his apartment or hers they lay on top of each other, sometimes fully dressed, their legs sticking off the bed, various body parts cracking and creaking and crushed, the two of them imbricated like a poorly laid roof. As long as they didn't talk, they walked through the deep grass, they heard how it buzzed in summer. They held each other for warmth in winter, then put on their skates and flew.

It was a form of worship that the cantor had for this lady, and though she asked for nothing, he brought her offerings anyway. Because she accessorized only in blue and green, he would have liked to give her opals and emeralds. Instead the rings he gave her were fake, so fake that the stones didn't even have names. The earrings he gave her dangled with plastic baubles. She was the only woman in the world around whom he was shy, and he was never shier than when he handed over one of these treasures, which he had personally wrapped fancy, as if it had come from Cartier instead of Kmart. When she took it she laughed. She opened the box to reveal its contents and threw back her head and roared, and this confused him, for she immediately put on whatever it was and she always looked marvelous in it.

The jewels may not have been real, but he took her on the kinds of dates that a banker might have—if, that is, the banker happened to be classy in addition to rich. In the downtown there was an art museum in an old mansion; there was no art in this museum, only furniture, but once a month there was a film. They saw *Lawrence of Arabia* there, and *Doctor Zhivago*. Whenever an opera singer performed at the Civic Center the cantor and Leah were there. Sunday mornings they went to the delicatessen and swooned before the case, with its golden whitefish and coral lox, its eggplant salads and bricks of halvah, its ruby meats delivered from Atlanta. They tasted this and that and they never left empty-handed.

They enjoyed themselves, and Leah never realized how much it cost him. The desperateness of his life was a secret

to her. At the Civic Center he went the day of the show to get
tickets; there were last-minute deals. The balcony was cheaper
than the orchestra. Certain seats were behind a column and
these were the cheapest of all. So many ways, none of them
ending in a very good look at the performer. At least they had
a little meat on them, most of these singers, and so a front-row
seat was not required. At least they knew how to project, and
the acoustics in the auditorium weren't the worst.

And then it came time to buy tickets for Beverly Sills, who
though she had recently retired was coming to give a benefit performance. Beverly Sills (née Belle Silverman) was a star
who gave him and all Jews such *naches*, he intended to have a
good look at her. Half his congregants were certain to be there
that night, so if he went at the last minute he might not be able
to get tickets anyway—and he wasn't about to let them see a
man who usually sat before them elevated on an altar now sit
behind them or blocked by a post.

   And so he went a month in advance. He walked up to the
box-office window and saw his reflection in it. He was glad he
wore his good checked shirt and put on a tie; his hat was tilted
just right. Perhaps the success of his outfit was what made him
feel confident enough to say something he didn't even know
he was going to say. He took off his sunglasses and put his face
up close to the glass. Inside sat a young girl, blond and very
pretty, with dense brown freckles laid like a saddle across her
nose. "May I help you?" she boomed through the microphone
like the Voice of God Himself, and he took a step or two back.
"Yes," he said. "I would like to purchase your two best tickets to Miss Beverly Sills, the opera star." He had never asked
for the best tickets in his life, he had no idea how much they
cost. "Orchestra center, row D at the end?" she asked. "I'll
take them," he said. "By the way, miss, I am the cantor from

Congregation Beth Shalom. Please be kind to apply the clergyman's discount to my purchase." "What?" the girl asked.
"Clergyman's discount. For men of God. Like a reverend, my
dear." "You're a reverend?" "I'm a cantor. That means I sing.
I'm like a rabbi who sings. A singing rabbi. My life is devoted
to singing the praises of the Lord." Silently he was praying
she wouldn't bring up Jesus, a popular subject down here that
always left him at a loss. Instead she said, "We don't have a
clergyman's discount, sir." "What?" he asked with a shocked
expression. "I understand you have a military discount," he
said. "Yes, sir, are you a chaplain at Hunter?" "No, but tell me,
how many of our fine brave men from the air force base have
come to buy a ticket for Miss Sills?" "None that I know of,"
she said. "All right, my dear, then might a man of God, while of
course not as worthy as one of these fine young men, maybe one
of their tickets you'll give to me? Is two asking for too much—
one for me and one for, for the rabbi? Of course I'll surrender
mine if one of these young heroes wants a ticket, for my country I'll do this, but until then—" "I'll have to ask my manager,"
she said. When she came back she asked, "How many tickets
would you like, Reverend?"

The tickets were free. It was one of the greatest triumphs
of his life—but in the box-office window he saw how his forehead was glistening with sweat, and when he got home he had
to change his shirt.

There was also a story behind how he managed to obtain
his Sunday morning feasts with Leah, even though the price of
nova was out of this world.

The cantor wasn't interested in money, just what money
could get him, namely respect, both from the community, for
this was America, and from Leah herself, whom he would have
liked to hear not laughing at all when he handed her a gift.
Hear the sweeter laughter of a silence stunned with delight.

Leah loved him despite the meagerness of his pocketbook—
and so he wanted to reward her with something that truly was
worth something, a surprise ending as in a fairy tale.

With the money he saved from the Beverly Sills tickets the
cantor took Leah out to dinner. They never went out to dinner.
They couldn't, for there was no kosher restaurant in town. But
recently it had come to the cantor's attention that the rabbi and
rebbetzin had been seen dining at Opal's Southern Kitchen, a
seafood place on the way to the beach. The cantor crossed the
hall from his office to the rabbi's. He entered without knock-
ing, triumphantly confronting the rabbi with the news that
he, the rabbi himself, had been caught so flagrantly sinning.
The cantor left, however, with news of his own—how to have a
kosher meal at a *goyishe* restaurant.

The cantor suggested the idea to Leah. He thought she
would be shocked by his daring. But before he could explain
how it worked, she said, "Why not?"

They went on a Sunday evening, when all the other Jews
were eating Chinese. He asked for their flounder broiled on a
piece of aluminum foil. He asked that it be served on a paper
plate, he asked for plastic cutlery, he chose the side dishes:
baked potato, coleslaw, and corn. A picnic indoors! The food
was delicious, and Leah ate every speck of it, including what
might have found its way onto her fingertips. There could not
have been anything better, he agreed, except possibly what
flew by them with distracting regularity, one tray after another,
each laden with plates piled with hush puppies and French
fries. Now, this was the smell of the Garden of Eden, Leah's
head seemed to be saying as it swerved in the direction of each
passing tray, like a light-loving plant toward the sun.

But of course they couldn't eat anything fried. They didn't
trust the grease. They saw with their own eyes, the shrimp

and scallops and who knew what other kind of *trayf* nestled up against the fries on the passing plates as they may well have been arranged in the cooker itself, all of it swimming through bubbling oil like some strange school.

One evening, though, Leah left the table to touch up her face, and shortly after she returned, an order of hush puppies was delivered to them on a paper plate. They were shaped like turds. She popped one in her mouth and the cantor's blood flooded with a tremendous excitement. He must have looked shocked, for she stuck out her tongue at him.

"What," she said, "corn, it isn't kosher?"

"How does it taste?" he asked with amazement.

She closed her eyes and sighed.

"But what about the grease?" he asked.

"It's vegetable grease," she snapped. "I went in the kitchen and asked. Since when isn't a vegetable kosher?"

"But in it they put shrimp, in it they put—"

"I don't know anything about that." She put another hush puppy in her mouth and chewed. "Besides, at five hundred degrees, anything *trayf* gets killed."

"It smells good," he conceded.

She shrugged. "Eat it, don't eat it, do what you want."

II

The cantor saw the young lady around the shul, in the electric hum of the still afternoons. She was beautiful but a mouse. Maybe she didn't realize her beauty, maybe someone had harmed her in the past. Whenever he passed her in the lobby or noticed her in the main office she looked down and froze in place, like a child making herself invisible by closing her eyes. She was in the Sisterhood and had something to do with the Bulletin. He didn't know her name. One day she came up to him. Trembling, she told him his voice moved her to tears. He put his hand to his lips, then removed it and whispered, "Then I should remain quiet so that your beautiful eyes remain clear."

Then she disappeared. He no longer saw her in the main office, and she wasn't someone who regularly came to shul. Surely she was in the sanctuary on the High Holy Days, but so was everyone else. Two years later she reappeared, in his office, with a boy. The cantor seated her under a photograph of himself as a young cantor, his first portrait in America, which he had had colored and retouched; the boy he seated under the framed cartoon of The Man Who Burped in Shul on Yom Kippur. He was a good-looking boy, though like his mother two years earlier, he wouldn't look at you; he too seemed to want to disappear. He was wearing a white T-shirt and black jeans sawed off at the knees; his shoes were leather and black but his socks were white; his hair was a crazy nest of black curls. An interesting style, borrowed partly from an old man and partly from a child. He did not appear to have ever set foot in the sun, though outside, at that moment, if you so much as stepped outside without a hat you would burn up or at least turn *shvartz*. The kid had got himself up entirely in black and white—but the world happened to be in color, and so he stood out all the more.

"He speaks perfect Hebrew," the mother said.

"Not really," the boy clarified.

"And we never sent him to the day school," she said. "Just from what he learned in the afternoons. He picks it up. He writes Hebrew too. He loves to write—he's a wonderful writer. He writes stories, he writes poems, he writes song lyrics—just gorgeous. I actually got my associate of arts degree in English, and that wasn't too long ago. Everybody said what are you going to do with that, and I said, 'There isn't any major for being a housewife and mother unless it's Criminal Justice or Abnormal Psychology!'"

She was still a beautiful woman. And though she was more talkative than before, she wasn't really so different—the shyness and the nonstop talking opposite sides of the same coin. She was uncomfortable having a conversation, and when he interrupted to say something, she simply kept on. Finally, the cantor sent the boy out.

"My dear," said the cantor. "It's wonderful to see you again and to meet your son. I used to run into you in the office sometimes."

She looked down into her lap and tapped her feet. She looked up and said, "My association with the Bulletin has ended."

"I am sorry to hear that. I enjoyed seeing you."

"Thank you."

"The boy must keep you very busy."

She shook her head. "The editor and I had creative differences. I won't name names. Basically, I wanted to write articles and she wanted me to sell ads."

"Do you keep in touch with this editor?"

"Absolutely not. I haven't heard a word from her so I guess she found some other sap to sell the ads. That was really hard work—not that I minded doing it for the shul—but after three years I felt like I paid my dues. I consider myself a writer. A writer wants to write."

"Well," he said, "I'm sure you will have your chance, dear. In the meantime go home and write, write your words, write for yourself, that is the most important person, you, yourself, and you. As for the Bulletin, I'm happy to say something—"

"Oh no! I don't need that kind of aggravation. If you don't like me, then I'm not going to beg. She isn't the first and she won't be the last. But thank you, Cantor. Thank you so much."

———

Lesson number one. The cantor sat in the back row of the junior congregation room, as he always did with his students, who stood on the altar and sang for him. The cantor chose this row so that they couldn't see how distracted he was, though there was little chance of that. He seemed completely present—he didn't close his eyes, he knew how to swallow a yawn or jiggle his teeth to wake himself up—but in his head he was breathing in Leah's perfume, he was in bed with her or walking round the lakes over there. Now he was in the rabbi's house, in the living room where you had to take a step down to get to it, except instead of belonging to the rabbi the house was his, and instead of the rabbi's tasteless tchotchkes, some of them bordering on idolatrous—he had a little sad-faced rebbe he had picked up, along with a crystal candy dish, in a giftshop in the village of Auschwitz—the cantor had done it up the way he liked, with class.

But there was no sound anymore. The boy must have finished. He stood there in his black clothes as still as a cow and with great dark cow eyes. What this kid, whose father was an accountant, had to be sad about, the cantor didn't know.

"Have you picked out your bar mitzvah suit yet?" the cantor asked.

The boy nodded.

"And where did you go?"

"Levy's in the mall."

"Levy's in the mall. Very nice store, plus I had the Levy boy just last year."

The boy saw that next year the cantor would have forgotten his name too.

"So did you buy a suit?"

"Did I have a choice?"

"A comedian! Well, better than a tragedian. Did you buy a nice suit was what I meant."

"It's okay."

"It's okay. What was the mark?"

"What?"

"The brand, what brand did you get?"

"I don't know. Pierre Cardin, I think."

"Pierre Cardin. Pierre Cardin," the cantor repeated, savoring the beautiful French words. "Pierre Cardin is very nice."

The following week, when the mother came to pick up the boy, she came in again. Usually the mothers just waited outside in the car. The cantor invited her into his office, alone, and said, "I'm looking forward to working with your son. And I want to work out something with you on my rate."

"Your rate? You charge?"

"Only for what your dues don't cover. My dear, most of these boys, they just want to get it over with, they just want, frankly, to have a big party—and I won't say a little gelt in the pocket isn't an attraction for some too. I personally have nothing against a party. But when I meet a boy I see really wants to learn, who really wants to be a bar mitzvah, that's what I like to see. That's when I don't want to take anything at all. But normally I take, well— From you I'll take no more than twenty-five. Of course it's up to you."

She nodded, though he could see she didn't understand what he meant. What he meant was she could also pay nothing—but he bit his tongue instead of telling her. He watched her face change, he watched it relax. "Thank you," she finally said.

"Of course I wouldn't want to make the other parents jealous."

"No," she said seriously.

"Good," he replied. "Then you'll want to discuss it with your husband, dear?"

She laughed. "If you can make my son sound like you, my husband will pay anything!"

The cantor's face broke into a smile, his big teeth gleamed. He was surprised by how he felt, better than he thought he would.

One afternoon as the boy was singing, the cantor thought about how long it would take to save up enough for the necklace the saleslady at Siegel's had shown him. He had finally crossed the threshold of this store, in broad daylight, like any other paying customer. The necklace was a strand of gold hung with an emerald shaped like a teardrop. This image led him to an afternoon rendezvous with Leah, on the salmon-colored recamier in the ladies lounge, a deliciously dangerous fantasy that was spoiled by a honk. But there was no duck before him—just the kid, the strangely outfitted boy of the beautiful woman who, once prompted, couldn't stop talking about herself. A rude intrusion, this honk, but now the spell had been broken and there was no retracing his steps across the lobby. Even if he could get to the ladies lounge he would find his beloved gone, and who else in her place but Mrs. Fine or some other yenta in the stalls, making another kind of honk.

"Sing through your mouth," the cantor heard himself saying. "Not your nose."

The boy looked up, perplexed, not by the criticism but by the very fact the cantor was trying to teach him something.

"I'm not saying you got a beautiful voice," the cantor said.

The boy snorted.

"But try to remember what you are singing."

"I don't really have a clue."

"Then I'll tell you. You are singing holy words. Your voice should sound holy too."

"Uh, okay," the boy said skeptically.

The cantor stared. "Now, what about standing up straight?"

———

Every Thursday he saw the boy, then afterward the mother, alone in his office. The mother: powder, rouge, lipstick, hair, clothes, rings, nails, the smell of a rose. She looked like a vampire, a beautiful vampire, the beautiful victim of a vampire, with strategic places painted red to convey the impression of the living blood that the rest of her appeared to lack. But if she had been bitten, she remained the victim; she hadn't crossed over. He couldn't even see her swatting a fly, or he could see her trying but never managing to kill it. For a few minutes she talked, then reached into her beaded pocketbook and removed an envelope. She looked down as she passed it to him. He waited till she looked up and then slightly bowed his head and thanked her.

The cantor didn't tell Leah he was charging the boy's mother. He didn't plan to tell her when he gave her the necklace either. She never asked him such questions, there was no need to explain—though the fineness of this gift might cause her to wonder. That was okay. As long as she didn't laugh—even if it was only in the spirit of laughing with him—then she could do whatever she wanted. She could slap him on the *toches* and it would be fine with him. Even if she asked where the money came from, it would be fine, though he didn't know what he would say. It was true that having this secret from her was exciting. It wasn't just any kind of secret, it was, some might say, of a criminal nature. But he chose to think of it as a trespass not much worse than eating the hush puppies.

It was a question of knowing. He didn't really know what else was cooked in the grease with each batch of hush puppies, not being in the kitchen himself. He didn't know that what he took weekly from the mother wasn't just an advance on a tip he was going to get in the end anyway. Or should get—she was naïve, she probably didn't know about the tip in the first place.

———

"Now, don't sing down into your book, look at me and sing to me."

The cantor was sitting in the front row of the junior congregation room. With each lesson he had moved up a row.

The boy looked down at the cantor, then back at his book, then down at the cantor again. But as soon as the boy opened his mouth, before any sound emerged, the cantor called out, "Now, if you wouldn't mind, please, about the accent. Would it kill you, darling, to sound like you come a little closer near Eretz Yisroel? Try to get a little closer to the Mideast than the Southeast. Try a *resh*, *r*, *rishon*, the first, number one, numero uno. Open your mouth a little, smile wide, that's it, not too much, take the *r* from the back of the mouth, not the front, *rishon*, now the *shon*, not *oh*, not *ohoo*, but closer to *aw*, *rishon*, *rishon*, accent on the *shon*, *ri-SHON*, not *RI-shon*, which means what, reshown?, show again?, a car maybe, used?"

"Nobody ever cared how I sounded before," the boy said suspiciously.

"I care." And as he said it the cantor saw that it was true. "You should too."

The boy shrugged. Then he started to sing. He no longer honked, the sounds he was making emerged from his mouth rather than his nose. His Torah portion was set during the travels of the Israelites through the wilderness; it told of the uprising of three men against Moses and how they were swallowed up into the bowels of the earth. The boy sang as if he meant it. He had practiced so many times that he no longer needed to look at the words. The boy closed his eyes when he sang, and the cantor had the unexpected sensation of tears welling up.

Now when his girlfriend popped into the cantor's head it was as an unwelcome distraction. Not only did he no longer indulge these fantasies, he tried not to think of her at all during his lessons. But this was hard to do, because he had calculated he would have the money to buy the necklace around the same time that the boy had his bar mitzvah ceremony. The first time he had walked into Siegel's, the cantor could have walked out with the necklace. Siegel was not one of his congregants, he attended the Orthodox shul—and yet he came over and personally offered the cantor a discount, he suggested layaway, he did everything in his power short of handing over the necklace for free. To all offers the cantor said no. He asked only that the necklace be set aside until he could afford to pay for it in full, which turned out to be the end of June, when the boy would become a bar mitzvah as well.

The necklace was like something growing in secret, underground, blind and tuberous and dark; while the bar mitzvah the cantor was cultivating in full sunlight. But on the surface his life looked the same as it had before he started taking money from the boy's mother. He was on a first-name basis with the girl at the symphony box office, he pulled his strings to obtain the Sunday lox—the old tricks still worked, so why not use them? He even continued to bring Leah costume jewelry from Kmart. He wasn't trying to throw her off the scent, he didn't think there was a scent.

But he was wrong.

"So what's the matter with you?" she asked him one night.

They were sitting at Opal's before their empty plates.

"Why do you ask?" he said.

"Because you didn't eat a hush puppy. Not one. I ate all yours. I'm not complaining."

She was green as the forest, blue as the sea, red as fire and clay. She was a fantasia of primary colors, all the elements that make up the creation. Her lips glistening with grease only accentuated her strange earthy beauty. He pictured the necklace hanging amid all this splendor and found it unnecessary.

"I was thinking what next after the hush puppies." The cantor looked around, then said, in a whisper, "Shrimp?"

"Maybe!" she exclaimed, to his horror.

But she was teasing. She must have been. She must have liked confusing him.

"For you it's not a temptation," he said. "For me—"

She looked at him as if he were mad.

He wanted to tell all—that he had crossed over into transgression, that maybe this refusal of the hush puppy, this one step backward, would somehow set him back onto the right path. But then Leah would really think he was crazy.

"Okay, so don't eat the hush puppies," she finally said. "If you're hungry, take another piece of corn instead."

The food sat in him like a weight.

Afterward, they went back to her apartment. But as much as they tried—without a word between them—they couldn't get back to the lakes.

With still three weeks to go, the boy was prepared. He was never going to be a Caruso but he sounded as good as he was going to get. And who really cared how he sounded when he read Hebrew so well, when he sang with such heart and soul? So one day the cantor asked the boy to take a seat alongside him on the altar.

"We never talked about your parsha so much," the cantor said. "You're giving the *drash*, you have something you'd like me to listen to? Maybe some idea you have in your head? Don't tell the rabbi, he'll say this is his territory, but between you and me—"

"I've been thinking about it," the boy said. "Waiting for something to come to me."

"Because I have an idea. If it was me giving the *drash*—if they ever let a lowly cantor give one, I mean, which they never would—I think I would say something about miracles. Don't believe what they say in the movies. There aren't really so many miracles in the Torah. It's not every bar mitzvah that gets one."

The boy smirked.

"The earth opening up, the fires of hell, whoa, that's some miracle," the cantor said.

"Yeah, it's like an earthquake except it targets, like, three people."

"More. Their families too."

"Excellent," the boy said.

The cantor felt an anger rising up. "Why do you talk like this, you, my boy?"

"Because I don't believe in miracles."

"With all due respect I don't believe you. I hear you, every week I listen to you sing. I don't believe you don't believe in miracles."

The boy shrugged. "I want to believe in miracles. I could really use one at this point. I could probably use more than one."

The cantor felt a little afraid to know what the boy was talking about.

"But when was the last time a miracle happened?" the boy asked.

"You mean you have never seen one," the cantor replied.

"No, I haven't. And no one else has either."

"Some have," the cantor said. "I have.

So the cantor had something left to teach after all, and in fact it was one of the things he had been hired to teach. The bumpkins on the Board had encouraged him to tell his story—his story!—to anyone who asked, of any age, especially his bar mitzvah students. But the cantor didn't feel he was being compensated properly for one position, much less two; and besides, everyone knows a bird in a cage doesn't sing.

The boy looked at him.

The cantor started to sing.

"It was in a tree," the cantor said. "I was in a tree. It was a nice sunny day. The sky was blue. And then it started to rain."

The boy had the confused, guilty look of someone who's being reprimanded without knowing quite why.

"And that's it," the cantor said. "The man pointing the gun at me put it down. He shouted something at his dog and the two of them went away."

The air conditioning clicked on.

"This was long ago," the cantor said.

"And just because he didn't want to get wet he didn't shoot you?" the boy asked.

The cantor's chilling smile socked the boy no less than Miss Bodziner's curselike answers to his questions in Hebrew class. "You wanted he should shoot me?" the cantor asked.

"No!" the boy said. "It's just, I mean, he was a Nazi and all."

"You think it's better to get wet than to let someone live? Let me tell you, I understand perfectly this man. It's a wonderful thing to want to stay dry, to me it makes a perfect sense. I also would choose to stay dry than to, God forbid, murder a Jew, if given the choice. For this reason I personally carry my umbrella with me at all times, even on a sunny day. Do you trust the weather report? Not me!"

And this didn't seem like such a joke, the cantor with his hair slicked back and sprayed in place, with his always shined shoes, no, he wouldn't like to get wet.

III

The constellations in heaven wheeled toward the appointed moment when the holy words must be read, when these particular ones must be read, while at the same time, underground rivers of lava tumbled and crashed, forging in their beds gold and precious stones. Everything happened at the same time, the entire universe heading toward a single moment of revelation, all according to the divine plan. Speeding toward the moment—time moved faster the older he got, the cantor was familiar with this, but never had it moved with such delirious speed. Although man was but a speck of dust in the universe, he too was part of the divine plan, a humble actor in it.

He was a cantor, he walked out onto a stage and sang before an audience. He was only the most obvious actor in the plan, perhaps the only one aware of his role. But everyone had a part to play! The boy's mother came onstage and said, "You've done wonders for my son, Cantor. I used to worry, I really did, I worried about everything, even those shoes he wears with the white socks, I heard someone say it meant he was, well, you don't want to know what they said! I mean I asked, I guess I deserved to hear what they had to say, I must have wanted an answer or I wouldn't have asked. Ridiculous, isn't it, I mean who cares? And I've been thinking about what you were saying, that if I want to be a writer I should just go home and write instead of waiting for someone to ask me to write—or let me write. I don't need anyone's permission—I don't know why I thought I did."

She handed over the envelope with the check and now it was the cantor who looked down.

His girlfriend came on and said, "Please, we are all we have here, in this place of poisonous swamps and killing heat and stupid children and flying roaches and bloodsucking bugs, we must hold each other and love each other and not be so sad."

They were out of character and as a result that much more convincing, the cantor thought as these sweet words poured into his ears, and so why couldn't he get that window out of his head, why couldn't he shake his desire to smash and smash and smash?

The boy came on and, with his sad eyes closed, sang.

———

And now, one week before the performance, the dress rehearsal!
They were alone in the main sanctuary, the cantor in a sea of
pews, the boy on the deep altar, the twin heights of stained
glass on either side of the ark showing Jacob wrestling with the
angel. The boy sang and the cantor moved from place to place,
to test the acoustics, a luxury he had never had with his other
students, who up to a day before the bar mitzvah were still trying to memorize their parts from a recording.

"You can sing louder," the cantor called out from the back
row. "Don't be afraid!"

The boy complied.

The cantor finally settled in a spot directly before the boy,
three rows back. In his black suit and white shirt the boy was
for once wearing the right shoes; he had even tamed his curls
and allowed the shaved side of his head to grow out a little. He
looked right up there, like a man, and the cantor felt everything
was going to be fine. But instead of the few moments of peace
the boy's voice usually brought him, the cantor saw Aaron
and Moses pleading with the enraged Lord not to destroy the
Israelites, not to kill them all. And the Lord agreed and sent
Moses, though he couldn't speak well, to stand before the people and predict the miracle and warn the righteous to move out
of the way. And now it was happening, the earth cracking open
and closing like a mouth, swallowing up the three rebels and
their families.

Now it was over and the Jews could move on.

For this was the miracle—not the swallowing up but the
moving on. A story of salvation, not of destruction: this was
what the boy, self-blinded, revealed. Some had to die so that
others might live. We are all of us standing on the fault, but it
is for each of us to choose to stay—or step away.

The cantor sat trembling with terror and awe.

Why was the boy disclosing this now, now that the cantor

had already, in his head, stepped away? Today was the final lesson, today he would receive the last check—and afterward it would be over and he could go back. He wouldn't touch the check, he would take it and put it in his desk drawer. If that would leave the accountant father's books suspiciously out of balance, the cantor would deposit the check but not touch the money. Or he would touch the money—but only to give it to charity. He would give it all to charity, everything that the mother, that trusting soul, had given him—for he hadn't yet spent a penny on the necklace and he didn't intend to. He would tell Siegel the deal was off. Then he and Leah could get back to the lakes.

When the lesson was over he resisted taking a shortcut through the rabbi's office, though the rabbi wasn't in. With the boy following, the cantor walked down the central aisle of the sanctuary, speeding up as he approached the lobby, racing across the slick floor in his white robe like a determined ghost, then bursting into the junior congregation room. The mother's perfume was in the air. Never had scent smelled so sweet! With a blinding smile stretched across his face he threw open his office door. She wasn't there. But of course she wasn't. She probably didn't know they were practicing in the main sanctuary today, she had come to the junior congregation room to find it empty and had left.

Then he saw that something had been left behind: an envelope in the center of his desk. He tore it open to get at the check, which he would never spend and which as a result was all the more valuable, his ticket to the future itself.

But inside there was just a note, no, a letter, both sides of the page covered by a tiny scrawl. Even when he shook the envelope no check fell out—and when he turned around the boy was gone.

The cantor ran to the front door of the synagogue and pushed it open. He saw the back of the mother's Cadillac heading away down the drive. The cantor jogged alongside the car, he wanted to say a word, only one! But as the passenger window flowed by, he saw only his own ashen face.

Back inside the cool gloom of the lobby the cantor found he still had the note in his hand. He squinted to make out the words.

Dear Cantor,

Last week I ran into Elise Epstein at the synagogue when I came to pick up my son. She was here to pick up her son too, who as you know is in my son's bar mitzvah class. I happened to mention how much you've been doing for my son. That's right, I praised you—and I meant every word of it. I didn't mention how much you were charging me, I promised you I would not. But I did happen to make a joke about what a bargain it was, considering how far my son had come. She said she didn't know what I meant. I thought she meant that because her son is not as exceptional as mine, no amount of singing lessons would do any good, no matter how much they cost.

That isn't what she meant.

You aren't charging Elise or Arlene Goodman or Natalie Berens or Etta Friedman or Bathsheba Blum. I know because I called them all, even the ones I don't know so well, even the ones who high-hat me when I run into them, and it was awkward and it hurt. But sometimes the truth hurts.

The blood drained from his fingers, the note was in danger of falling to the floor—but he held on to it.

I intend to get my money back. And I intend to stop you from victimizing anyone else—if you can find anyone as dumb as I was. That's why I'm going to the Board. Who knows, maybe they already know, considering everyone else does. I don't care if I'm a laughingstock, I don't care what people think of me, not anymore. At this point the only one I care about is my son. Which is why I'm not going to the Board until after his bar mitzvah. It will be the most beautiful event anyone has ever seen. I've planned it all to perfection, from the flowers on the bimah to the pastry selection for dessert. And you will be up there with my son who adores you. You can pack your bags and leave town the day after, for all I care. But it is my son's special day and I want him to be none the wiser.

I don't know what will be going on in your head. But I'm not letting you out of my sight. And if you look out at me, you're going to see a woman ruining her makeup crying. I will be crying at the miracle I've produced, the miracle that a son like this could come from someone like me.

I'm not talented. I don't think I write like Isaac Bashevis Singer, and you could give me a hundred lessons and you still wouldn't want to hear me sing! I'm not educated, not really. But I have learned enough Hebrew to say the Shabbat prayers. I have learned enough to make a decent Jewish home for my family, a home where we put our Jewish principles into practice, where we would never take advantage of anyone the way—

"What a day," the cantor heard his Leah say as she approached.

He started to stuff the letter into his pocket—but for what reason, now that everything had been revealed?

The lights in the office were dark, the secretary had gone home, and they both knew they were alone in the synagogue.

"Nu?" she asked.

His smile had returned but it no longer blinded.

"And what are you reading?" she asked.

"Something. From the boy's mother."

Leah raised a perfectly drawn eyebrow. "A love letter?"

The cantor shook his head. "A thank-you note."

THE GOLEM

I

In Solomon Blaustein's personal cosmology, the dealer stood at the bottom. The excrement of everyone else, virtuous ones and other demonic types as well, dropped onto the dealer's head. With his access to brand-new certified quote-unquote standard parts, priced to eliminate any profit that Blaustein or any other hard-working American small businessman might hope to make, the dealer believed himself to be a god. But a gulf lay between image and reality.

Blaustein got parts elsewhere. A Jew named Herman Lefkowitz, who had turned his father's junkyard into an impressive "metal recycling" business, supplied them. Actually, he did nothing so active as that, having pioneered something called Pick and Pay—there had been legal troubles with the shoe outfit of a similar name but Lefkowitz had won—in which the customer searched for the part he needed among rows of junked cars. The cars themselves didn't get fed into Lefkowitz's state-of-the-art recycling machine until they had been drained of all fluids and stripped of every part of value. Lefkowitz needed no one on his payroll for this; customers paid for the privilege.

Usually Blaustein called ahead. Lefkowitz took his calls—but they went always the same way. After a long and pointless conversation in which Blaustein inquired and Lefkowitz hedged and Blaustein begged and Lefkowitz laughed and Blaustein threatened and Lefkowitz cursed before finally admitting he had no idea what the hell was in his yard, he just wanted his old friend Blaustein to come over and have a cup of tea or some schnapps with him, Blaustein sighed. Lefkowitz was rich, he could afford to sit all day on a toilet and read the paper if he wanted to. Blaustein could not. He hung up and drove over to the yard. He tried to sneak past Lefkowitz. His office in this place of destruction was done up to look like a little house, made of cinderblocks painted yellow, with a white picket fence and even a rosebush, and if Blaustein crouched below the window with its open dollhouse shutters he was usually home free, at least until he had found his parts and it was time to pay. It was a hell of a way for Blaustein to run his business.

Where Lefkowitz stood in Blaustein's cosmology was high. He hadn't worked it out completely, but this was a charitable man whose scales, as far as Blaustein knew, were true. Where he himself, Solomon Blaustein, stood in his own personal cosmology was not up to him to say. Nor would it be to any man of himself. Not at the top, not as high as Lefkowitz—but nowhere near the bottom where the dealer with his shit head stood.

Blaustein had three mechanics working for him. They took the parts that came from the yard, cleaned them up, and installed them in the cars where they were needed. This was Blaustein's business. You could say he had others working for him as well, though they were not on his payroll. There was a fat blond girl named Shirlene and a skinny black girl named Tanyetta who worked as dispatchers at AAA, and at

Christmastime he always sent a little something their way. There were four cracker adjusters—three affiliated with insurance companies, one independent—to whom he supplied the finest in whiskey, and not just at Christmas. The whiskey Blaustein himself fetched, from a place of perfect order and cleanliness in the historic district that was named the Crystal Decanter and owned by a goy.

Because of his many absences, Blaustein's business, he felt, was always on the verge of collapse. He had no evidence of this, and in fact, as his accountant observed and he himself would announce to anyone who asked, business was booming. But the distance between boom and collapse was not so great. On a nature program he had seen that a Chinese bird's nest was held together with spit. Or you could take the example of a house of cards. In his business Blaustein supplied the spit; he was the card at the very bottom of the house that if removed would bring the entire structure toppling down. It was his name on the front of the building and the sides of the tow truck. And if you pulled into his garage nowadays, there was no guarantee he would even be there. Instead a mechanic, who might or might not be stealing from the business, would lift his head out of the hood of a car and make you wait until he was done. Finally, this greasy-handed person would ask what you wanted, whereas any good businessman knew you didn't ask the customer what he wanted, you told him.

Here in the "men's sports area" of the Jewish Educational Alliance, a brownness pervaded everything—the lockers, the medicine ball, the punching bag, the cracked and taped-up vinyl massage table, and everywhere the light that had no visible source and appeared to be filtered through wastewater. Airless, humid, hot, fragrant with the activity of a million microorganisms, the place had much in common with a sewer, although unlike a sewer, this was a place where a man could be bent, stretched, karate-chopped, and kneed into submission.

Blaustein had come here to relax. The masseur was a man named Martin—no one called him by his last name—who wore thick-framed Coke-bottle glasses and a kind of medical orderly's outfit and the goofy smile of a simpleton. He was a universal object of mockery and yet was known to have a firm touch. Blaustein nodded at Martin—you didn't shake this man's hand—and went to the lockerroom to disrobe. On his way in Blaustein saw his old friend Artie coming out. The stack of towels in Artie's hands almost completely covered his face, but Blaustein would have recognized him by his limp alone. For every three steps he took, his left foot took a break. The top half of his body lurched forward and with this momentum his right foot took a big step, and in this way Artie made it through the world, surprisingly fast.

It was because of this limp that Blaustein liked to keep an eye on Artie. Make no mistake—even before the attack, Artie had been a slow type of individual. Afterward, well— This was in the old neighborhood, a softball game that had gone on too long, crickets screeching around them, bats streaking past the treetops, and just then three Irish boys materializing out of the lane. You could barely see—but the biggest one said they wanted to play. Artie and the other Jewish boys turned to Sol, who was holding the baseball bat. What choice did he have but to hand it over? Would any one of them have done different?

Blaustein stopped and called Artie's name.

Artie turned around but didn't seem surprised.

"When did you start here?" Blaustein asked.

"It was. Let's s-s-see, it was—"

"What happened to Grossman's?" This was a local supermarket chain where Artie had had a job as a bagboy.

"They let me go last year."

"Goddamn that Grossman. What, he fired you because you weren't as fast as a kid? That's what you call age discrimination, you could sue. I'll call Stevie Goldberg, he'll know what to do."

"I don't know."

"Why don't you give me a massage."

"Okay."

"I mean, I can see you're like the golem here, with that Martin telling you what to do, but do you ever get to give a massage yourself? Don't you want to learn a trade?"

In fact Artie sometimes gave a massage. The fat ones, the ones bearlike with hairiness, those who had bad odors or poked at the sheet with an erect member—these were the clients that Martin gave him.

A few minutes later Artie was kneading Blaustein's muscles through his papery copper-colored skin. Blaustein turned his head to the wall, and though they were in a private room he spoke in a hoarse whisper. "Are you happy here?" he asked. And: "Is this what you want out of life?" He offered his old friend the chance to leave this underground world for a fresh-air job; to work in a more manly field; and to be his own man, albeit in the capacity of Blaustein's assistant.

Artie rarely spoke more than he needed to anyway. Still, Blaustein could tell from Artie's silence that he wasn't getting anywhere. "I haven't had a solid bowel movement in years," he said, letting the gas escape from under the sheet in illustration. "Food doesn't digest inside me, it rots. I buy Tums by the case at Kmart and that's what I eat instead of candy."

Artie seemed to be trying to pull Blaustein's leg out of its socket and he cried out.

"Ask me how I sleep," Blaustein said.

"Okay."

"I don't. But every night I try. I drink a NyQuil chased with a shot of slivovitz and sometimes I take a Valium if necessary."

Artie pulled Blaustein's arms straight back along his spine, and Blaustein muttered curses under his breath.

"Why?" Blaustein asked. "One word. Tension! I need help. Someone I can trust. An old friend. How long has it been since we've seen each other?"

"Last time was—" Artie snuck in almost before Blaustein had finished. "I don't know. I s-s-see you around."

The words *the* and *a*, Blaustein had noticed, caused Artie special trouble, and so he left them out, like a Russian. Also his timing was off. Whenever whatever he needed to say was in the bag, he said it. Or maybe it just came out. Otherwise he circled the words he had to utter, like a hawk after a mouse, and when he spotted one of them he dove for the kill. It was a shame, Blaustein thought, that the ambition and aggressiveness other men were able to dedicate to being a big success in life, this man harnessed it all just to say boo.

"How much?" Artie asked, wedging the two words into the tiny space he felt was his.

"I've mentioned the perks."

"I'll t-t-tell you how much I make here."

"So that's it?" Blaustein asked, his voice rising. "That's all you're interested in?"

"Why not get a kid?"

"I've tried a kid. He wasn't responsible. Also a *shvartzer* I've tried. No good."

"What'll you pay me?"

Blaustein craned his neck up and around. "If that's all that matters to you, goddamn it, if that's how you talk to an old friend—"

"Hey," Artie said in a soothing voice, running his finger down Blaustein's spine. "You'll turn over now. You can look me in the face."

———

Where Artie fit into the cosmology, even the Lord Almighty would have had a hard time saying. In addition to his stutter and limp, his eyes pointed in different directions, like mis-aimed headlights. He got a disability check, which enabled him to survive on his salary from the discontinuous string of part-time and unreported shit jobs he had had over the years. Once Blaustein had seen Artie by the side of the road spearing garbage and putting it into a sack, though he wasn't wearing an orange vest or anything else that would distinguish him from a *meshuggener*. It was rush hour and Blaustein didn't want to embarrass him by stopping anyway. It was hard to know what to do. When Blaustein ran into him at the JEA he was glad to see him employed, but anyone could do better than that, even a man like this.

Artie saw reason and came to work at the garage. Blaustein paid him fifty cents more an hour than he was making at the JEA. But who knew if this investment would pay off? Blaustein tried to keep the big picture in mind, though from the start Artie tried him. He didn't know the makes or models of cars; he didn't even own one himself. The first time Artie went to the scrap-yard by himself, it took him twice as long as it should have. Next to the yard was the dump and for some reason he had stopped there, in a dump. It was only because he was an old friend that Blaustein didn't fire him on the spot. Rarely in a businessman's life did a hiring opportunity permit the fulfillment of a mitzvah. But should a respect for the past outweigh one's responsibilities to the present? When is enough enough? Such weighty questions kept Blaustein up that night and the next.

Spenser Estates Metalry was named for the plantation that stood there in the years between the Revolution and the Civil War, after which the gray brick house with its porticos and ter-races and stables collapsed under the weight of neglect and the rice fields reverted to marsh. When Artie started working for him, Blaustein called ahead and, avoiding Lefkowitz, talked to the girl, who laughed when he called her pet names such as Pecan Pie and Brown Sugar. Blaustein asked if they had this or that part. The girl couldn't say what was left in which car, but she could tell him which cars they had. There was no way to reserve a part, so when Blaustein hung up the phone he shouted at Artie to go!

One of the mechanics had taught Artie how to pry out various parts without damaging them or the rest of the car. Blaustein sent him for everything big and small: seatbelts, the rod that held up the hood, a door handle, mirrors, a fuel gauge, entire engines. Artie did as he was told. Blaustein came into the shop one morning feeling different, and it took him a while to realize he had fallen asleep the night before without drinking his NyQuil. He had slept almost till dawn. When Artie came in he was about to embrace him—but then he saw he was carrying a grocery bag. "What's this?" Blaustein asked. "A big lunch?" "Headlights," Artie replied, opening the bag. "I can see what they are," Blaustein said. "Who the hell authorized you to get them?" "We always need headlights. Th-th-these are compatible with—" "They're compatible with," Blaustein said mockingly. "Who told you that, a little birdie? Don't tell me, Lefkowitz!" he cried, seeing in his mind the junk man falling from his heights to that metaphysical place where rich charlatans and thieves dwelled.

Still, it was Artie he blamed. He damned him to hell. He gave him a choice—either pay for the lights out of his own pocket or watch his crippled *toches* get tossed out onto the street. But when that very afternoon Tanyetta the AAA dispatcher called him with a wreck just a few blocks away in the historic district, an Oldsmobile stationwagon in need of new headlights (among other parts), Blaustein told Artie he was lucky, he was given a reprieve and might not need to return as that *faygeleh* Martin's golem and apprentice *faygeleh*, if, that is, the position was still even open.

Soon Blaustein stopped calling the scrapyard ahead of time. Artie took on the job of going out to the yard first thing each morning, just to see any new cars before they were picked over, in case there was something worth taking. After only a few months he had developed such an eye that when he came back empty-handed, Blaustein could be sure there was nothing to get. In the summer Artie returned with air-conditioning units, naturally, but also with bumpers and grilles and headlights and those auto body parts that were most likely to need replacing after an accident on the highway down to Florida or up to the Blue Ridge. Blaustein had no place to store these parts and certainly wasn't going to lay out a dime to rent a space. But Artie had the knack for knowing what to bring in when, so that parts were available when they were needed and nothing sat around for more than a week. So that Blaustein rarely had to appeal to that most hated of figures, the dealer.

II

Demon shriek of metal tearing metal, stink of burned meat, turd heaps of fanged beasts that patrolled the yard by night. The scrapyard agreed with him. The Dobermans in their cage nudged him with their muzzles. The machine that swallowed cars and streamed sorted metals was interesting to watch. The hotdogs were Isaac Gellis. Here a junked car was a treasure chest. Here the men, some of them, who came to pick and pay were no finer physical specimens than he was. Armed with a box of tools, every man, no matter how lame or sound of leg or tongue, had the same challenges of finding what he was looking for and prying it out. It was hard manly work. Various parts of Artie's body were early casualties. Acids splashed along his arm, transmission fluid spurted into his eye. Fingers bent back and wedged in, tendons and muscles strained, and once even an eternity of fear when he lay poking at the undersides of a car and the car, which like every other one in the yard was not jacked up but instead balanced on welded rims, began to topple.

Artie was even threatened with violence. One day he had his head under the hood of a Plymouth Valiant; the man next to him was under a LeMans. It was only eight in the morning but already so hot and humid that Artie's eyes stung. The man next to him was a blur—a red blur on top of his head, a blur of dark hair covering his face, a blur of pale blue denim going down. Artie kept at his task but noticed something pink going down into the blue. He turned and saw the man's hand sticking one spark plug into the front of his jeans and then another.

"Hey!" Artie said.

The man in the red cap looked down at him. Then he ducked his head back into the engine.

"You have to p-p-pay," Artie said.

"Oh yeah?" the man said, his head still under the hood.

"Yeah," Artie confirmed. "T-t-twenty cents each."

"Is that right?" The man reached down under the car and rose up hugely, holding a tire iron over his head.

Artie blocked his head.

"You ever come across a car that someone died in?" the man asked.

Artie peeked through his arms. The man set the tire iron on the engine block.

"You come across it from time to time," the man said. "Bloodstains on the interior and bits of bone and hair and whatnot. Now I don't think that's right, putting a car that somebody died in on display like that. What do you think?"

Artie tried but nothing came out.

"Cat got your tongue?" the man asked.

"N-n-n—" Artie tried.

"Want me to fucking waste you in this car?" the man said, grabbing the tire iron again as Artie, in his hobbling way, fled. "Because I *will* waste you," the man shouted after him, "you ree-tard, you bitch."

It was a rude apprenticeship but it had passed. Artie learned how to locate and extract parts so quickly that he had time to feed the birds at the dump and be back before Blaustein even expected him. The dump had its own smells, of course, but also its own shrieks—the seagulls that dropped straight down onto the mountains of garbage as if they were attached by string and pulled by an invisible hand. They were aggressive, swarming Artie as soon as he stepped out of the truck. Every now and then a wading bird hopped out from among the trees, pecking at the mist that lay like manna on the ground. The gulls set upon the outsider but Artie shooed them away, sometimes with a rock, and made them wait their turn. Finally, he shook out ends of challah and crusts of sliced rye, he laughed when the birds closed in around him.

But Artie didn't like going to the Crystal Decanter, though it was easy, a cinch, involving neither picking nor paying. Here it was a reversion to the days before self-service; staff outnumbered clientele. And though Artie prepared something to say before he went in, practicing *p*'s and *f*'s and making sure he never even had to attempt an article, he rarely had to say a word, for after the first time he went in, his ongoing mission was known to the employees, who treated the agent of Blaustein like the emissary of a king. Several times during the year Artie left with cases of good whiskey; before holidays bottles were wrapped individually, in gold boxes and bags of purple velvet tied with a gold rope. But the very fact that he didn't have to talk announced how hard it would have been for him, there in that place where the bright light illuminated the grease stains on his clothes. Where every one of his imperfections was magnified in the mirrored walls, the cut-glass decanters and silver trays everywhere, the chandelier that hung in the middle of the room.

What did the Crystal Decanter have to do with the garage anyway? Artie always left the place, nice as it was, with a confusion in his head. The parts from the scrapyard went into the cars. The bottles from the liquor store got locked up in the metal cabinet in the office. But that cabinet like all others was finite in space. The bottles went in but Artie never saw them going out, and this made his head hurt even more. Blaustein should have had two assistants, Artie muttered in the truck. He should have been two men.

When Artie wasn't schlepping used car parts or fine spirits, he stood around the garage waiting. Blaustein spent his days talking to clients and insurance adjusters in his office, so Artie stayed on the garage floor, watching the mechanics. Inevitably one day one of them asked him to hand him a wrench. Soon what Artie had learned to take out, he believed he had learned to put in, though he had never tried it himself. Prying out parts had taken time to learn. Artie believed that putting parts back into cars, once he actually began doing it, would also take time to learn but could not possibly be as hazardous as the other way around.

"Since when do you have the experience to be a mechanic?" Blaustein asked.

Artie was standing in the office with the door closed. Blaustein was looking over his bifocals at a bill.

"S-s-since I started working with you," Artie said.

"As what? A mechanic? Or a golem that I send to a junkyard?"

Artie began to pace.

"Sure, help the guys out if you want, I don't care," Blaustein said. "But you can't expect me to pay you. I'm a small business-man and practically a senior citizen."

"We are s-s-same age."

Blaustein used a tanning light to control his psoriasis, an archipelago of pink ashy-beached islands in the orange sea of his forehead and neck. And so it was hard to tell when the tidal wave of angry blood rolled across his face. But Artie could tell, flinching even before Blaustein opened his mouth. "Goddamn you," Blaustein said to his face. "Goddamn you to hell. I'll fire you today."

"Hey, wait a minute."

"No, you wait a minute. If you think you're going to put me in the poorhouse— I put up with all that dreck you bring back from the yard, but a man has his limits."

There was a rapping at the door and through the milky security glass Blaustein appeared to recognize his visitor. He opened the door and there stood a young man in a pale blue short-sleeve shirt and yellow tie. He wore khakis and brown dress shoes. He had pens in his shirt pocket and carried a clip-board. "Mr. McCloskey!" Blaustein exclaimed, putting his arm around the young man. "Mr. Blaustein," McCloskey said, a lit-tle bashfully. Artie saw no way to escape and so he stood there, trembling with rage and trying to think of something to say if he needed to.

Blaustein escorted McCloskey in and told Artie he could go.

Artie sat at the desk outside Blaustein's office. It was no one's job to sit here, though everyone kept an eye on it, since this is where anyone who came into the garage would go first. Blaustein didn't like Artie to sit here. Artie sat anyway, watching the two shadows on the other side of the door. Murmur of voices, louder laughter. The adjusters were treated like dignitaries here, and not just by Blaustein. The mechanics deferred to them, maintaining a respectful distance. They never said a word against them, though the adjusters did little more than circle the cars they were adjusting, scribbling on their clipboards. But no new cars had been brought in today.

The door opened. McCloskey left with his clipboard and, cradled in the other arm, a paper bag.

A few months later, Blaustein called Artie into his office. Blaustein put the bottle of bourbon that Artie himself had fetched on the desk between them. Artie remembered it because it wasn't one of the brands of liquor he usually brought back. It had not come in a gold box. A black bird perched on the label. "Sure, I'll take a little," Blaustein said. "Happy Chanukah. You've earned it."

Artie opened the bottle and Blaustein took out two glasses from his desk drawer and poured. "L'chaim," he said.

"L'sholom," Artie warily replied.

They drank and Blaustein refilled their glasses. He leaned back in his chair and put his alligator shoes up on the desk.

"Yep, we did all right," Blaustein announced. "Two boys from the Twenty-seventh Street School, that's what we were. And here we are. I'm sitting on this side of the desk and you're sitting on the other, but we both ended up in the same place. And that's all right. To each according to his talents, to each according to his— I think that was in the Torah. Go ahead, I'll have another little drop."

Blaustein nodded at Artie to pour.

"This is a great business, isn't it?" Blaustein went on. "You know you really help me. You're a wonderful golem. I'm kidding you! But I can spend more time with the adjusters now. I love that McCloskey. Scotch is what he likes to drink.

Single-malt Scotch whiskey. Personally, I like bourbon. The sweetness of it. But compared to a goy, what does a Jew know about liquor? Single-malt Scotch. Well, he earned it. That last job, twelve hundred dollars is what it came in as, and I did it for under three. And people wonder why their insurance premiums are so high."

Artie cocked his head like a dog. "So that's why."

"Hah? What are you implying?"

"I'm not implying nothing. You said people wonder why th-th-their insurance premiums are so high."

"What did you say to me? I didn't say that."

A confusion was in Artie's head, it expressed itself on his face. He stared at the walls, which were covered with naked-lady calendars and Chamber of Commerce plaques and pictures of Blaustein with local bigwigs in front of the custom cars he procured for the St. Patrick's Day parade.

"Are you accusing me of being a ganef?" Blaustein asked. "Go ahead, yes or no? Is that what you think of me?"

"I'm n-n-not accusing. Just understanding."

"Do you think I can pass along those costs to my customers?" Blaustein asked. "Sure, maybe once—then I'll never see them again. Do you think I can make a profit that way? What do you think pays your salary?"

Artie sat there feeling his brain move in the sea inside his head.

"I don't even know why I'm arguing with you," Blaustein went on. "You don't have a clue, you putz. You have no idea how the world works. How could you? Do you think all of my competitors don't do the same thing? If I started sending you to the *dealer*," he said with disgust, "how would I be able to compete? Is everyone bad and you're the only one honest in the world? Is that really the way that little brain of yours works?"

The brain, the sea—Artie couldn't get anything out.

"Frankly, I think you're a little spooky," Blaustein said. "Don't they say golems have supernatural powers? How is it you know what accident is going to happen before it does? Hah? I don't know if I should report you to the police or what."

But now they were stirring, the words, swimming up through the thick dark water and into the light. "Go ahead."

There's Hope for Us All

Angelo Veneto, painter of young gentlemen, was having his first one-man show. It had taken nearly five hundred years. "Only five hundred years," Adger Boatwright liked to say. "I guess there's hope for us all!"

Adger Boatwright was the curator of Atlanta's Harrington Collection and he tried out the joke on each of the Ladies of the Board. It was the Ladies' Coca-Cola money that had paid for the Collection's Twenty Renaissance Gems, which included Angelo's portrait, circa 1515, of a smooth-cheeked young nobleman with a Mongol cast to his eyes and a dangerous gaze. The tail feathers of the canary are completely stuffed in this cat's mouth, sealed by a mildly belligerent smile. He's gripping a fat stick—say anything and he'll use it on you, though really he'd rather not. The Ladies were famously particular but *Portrait of a Gentleman in a Red Cape* was an easy sell. "Just *look* at him," Adger said to them, one at a time, in the darkness of the Collection's screening room. Each lady stared at the larger-than-life-size projected image, but Adger never took his eyes off the lady. He could see the fear in her, he could see she couldn't turn away. "Do you not find him beautiful?" he asked.

His powers of persuasion were such that the director of the Harrington gave him full access to the Ladies. Curators and directors could be water and oil, but Adger's interest in greasing the machinery that made the Collection run rivaled that of his boss, who complemented his curator's efforts by spending weekends golfing with the Ladies' husbands. Even if he could have afforded it, Adger would never have been admitted to the Club.

He was a large doughy man whose parents had met on the assembly line of the fruitcake factory in Claxton. He made it through the trial of high school by spending weekends with "friends" in nearby Savannah, where he was really being educated in pederasty, neoclassical American *objets*, and the magic of the society portrait. By the time he obtained his degree in art history from Emory, his accent was a liquid Low Country and the fruitcake-assembling parents no longer figured into his family story or his life. (A somewhat ruined but functioning silk plantation on the coast did appear in the boyhood part of the story, and no one ever pointed out that by the end of the eighteenth century the hope in silk had declined; by the end of the nineteenth, the silk plantations had all burned to the ground; and by the middle of the twentieth, the remaining mulberry trees were cut for timber, the dispossessed blue-blood silkworms obliged to fend for themselves.) Pederasty too had fallen away, in favor of innuendo and art. The Ladies loved Adger most especially because he never brought *it* up. He had a way about him that made it easy for them to agree with a *man* that yes, the taunting young aristocrat in the painting was, mercy, beautiful. A decade later, when the idea for the one-man show was taking shape and Adger told the joke to the Ladies—there were three more of them by now—they all laughed, and one by one removed their checkbooks from their purses.

———

Jonathan Weitz had overheard the joke four times already, and he did not think it was funny. For two years he'd been the Collection's associate curator and still had no office, just a desk outside Adger's enormous portrait-lined room. Jon sat behind a half wall that revealed his head and yet made him invisible to the director whenever he came to see Adger. The half wall was topped by a ledge that Adger leaned on as he made demands of Jon and fraught small talk. The best Jon could do was fake a laugh when Adger, after escorting out one of his Ladies, tried the joke on him.

It wasn't the extravagance of Adger Boatwright's closet that bothered Jon, nor even the fact of it. It hadn't been so long since that freezing New Haven night when Jon walked around the Old Campus half a dozen times before seeking out the college's Counselor of Homosexuals, who sat in a former chapel, waiting. As for Adger's insistence on self-invention, even if he had no talent for it—well, why not? No, what annoyed Jon was that Adger Boatwright, curator of the Harrington Collection, keeper of the Twenty Renaissance Gems, knew nothing about art. Oh, he loved beautiful paintings, especially portraits, especially when hung in a room full of exquisite furniture, preferably in England. But it was this very appreciation of a painting that blinded him to it.

A painting's provenance—who had owned it, where it had been shown, how much it had sold for at which auction house—fascinated Adger so much that it had given him the idea for his most recent show at the Harrington. Adger had chosen from the Collection the five paintings with the ritziest pasts. Antonio Boltraffio's *Portrait of a Lady with Pearls* was displayed alongside a gratuitous and absurd model of the parquet-floored room of the "English treasurehouse" where it had hung until the collection was dispersed after the Second World War. There were fingernail-sized paintings on its walls. Giorgione's *Portrait of a*

Girl—owned by the Duke of Edinburgh! The show was reso-
lutely anti-intellectual, its tone dizzily self-congratulatory. *A
Picture Is Worth a Thousand Words* was coming down just as Jon
got there but the museum was still abuzz; it was the most popular show in the history of any similar-sized institution in the
country. Adger was golden and insufferable.

Part lightweight travelogue, part flimsy mystery story,
part *This Old House*, the show had so much *stuff* in it that you
could easily overlook the paintings themselves. After an hour
alone with his new boss's show, Jon wondered if this wasn't the
point. Great art was easier not to look at than to truly take in.

In graduate school he had been considered old-fashioned,
and in a fusty field like art history this was saying something.
Like the Victorian poet and critic Matthew Arnold, Jon
believed the role of criticism was to illuminate the work of art
itself. His doctoral research on Pope Urban VIII was sound,
but he used it not to examine the nature of papal patronage but
instead to appreciate the marvels the pope had commissioned—
the churches, the sculpture, the loggias, the frescoes. The gift
of man's creation to the city—this was the sacred thing, and
the pope knew it. Jon was young and at Yale, he was supposed
to be interested in poststructuralism, postcolonialism, post-
Lacanian psychoanalysis—something current, something
French. He could have pretended. Instead he became like an
actress who won't keep herself blond enough or thin enough;
his prospects in the academy dried up. He got interviews but
not jobs; then he stopped getting interviews.

It was for the best, he reminded himself. Unlike his peers
he was not begging for visiting lectureships at poverty wages.
He had been spared this particular set of humiliations. He
was glad to be working for someone who had never heard of
Foucault. And yet he was having a hard time sharing Adger's
vision of the museum of art as a museum of artifacts, a kind of
grandmother's attic full of interesting juxtapositions.

As for the joke—well, the show hadn't even happened yet and Adger Boatwright was already burying the paintings. Because the joke wasn't just dumb, it shut out the truth, or at least the pursuit of it. Why had it taken Angelo Veneto five hundred years to get a show together? Never mind that the very idea of a show, a retrospective, was a modern one—presumably Adger knew that. Angelo was no Leonardo but he was as good as his more-famous contemporaries Bellini and Giorgione, who may have invented the modern portrait—the portrait that reveals "character" and "personality"—but never took it as far as Angelo did. Look at a Giorgione portrait and you think *This kid's head is in the clouds.* Or: *He's looking at me but he seems very far away.* And you feel secure in going further: just as you can't *not* read a billboard that suddenly looms before you, you can't help knowing what Giorgione's subjects are thinking. *How out of sorts I feel today! How life weighs on me in my youth! How strangely* nice *it feels to have Holofernes's head under my foot!* Captions suggest themselves. But the visual expression of specific thoughts wasn't the point; introspection itself became the subject of these paintings.

That was enough of an accomplishment for Giorgione—but not for Angelo. You want to shield your face, not guess what his subjects are thinking. Painted in three-quarters view, they stare at you or just beyond—they seem to have a secret they're daring you to figure out. They stand armed before landscapes; scraps of text hang and curl. You stare until you lose yourself in this labyrinth of symbols, which come into the painting from the usual places—family history, classical myth, the Bible—and emerge as elements of the subject's psyche. Spend time with the subject of the Collection's *Portrait of a Gentleman in a Red Cape* and you suspect his arrogance masks something that he'd rather not confront and that you too should avoid. He knows you're looking at him, he'll tolerate that. But if he knew you were focusing on the worn white codpiece appearing in the hole cut out of his black tunic—where the eye is naturally drawn, where it is impossible not to look—he wouldn't hesitate to use his stick on you.

You're lured, trapped, threatened, shamed—all at once. At least this was how Jon felt. Caravaggios affected him with their mysterious play of shadow and light, the gorgeous embattled flesh offering itself up to you—but when faced with, say, some street urchin pretending to be St. John the Baptist, Jon could never quite get past responding *No, you're not!* The Angelos affected him as no paintings ever had. How could he hold a light up to these paintings, as he was charged to do, when they seemed intent on his submission? It was distracting. It was nuts. No wonder Angelo Veneto had never had a retrospective: the last thing you'd want to do is end up in a room full of these things.

Adger Boatwright obviously thought otherwise. The Ladies went for that first Angelo because he had them focus on the painting's beauty to the exclusion of all else. Sure, he looks like he's going to kill you, but so what? He's Italian, and hot! Maybe Adger truly thought the sexiness of Angelo's paintings trumped all else. Whatever his attitude, thinking had little to do with it. The idea of the show had come to him in a vision. At the Louvre—where else? He was standing before the *Portrait of a Boy with a Hammer*, one of that museum's two Angelos, and he imagined all the painter's subjects crowding around him. Their various props—hammer, staff, horse-head sword—clattered and swung.

An Angelo Veneto show. It may have been a good idea—but how to pull it off?

The paintings are difficult, they generate a sense of unease—but there was another problem with mounting an Angelo show: almost nothing is known about him. Where and when he was born: no record. Where and when he died: ditto. His signature, on those paintings he signed, usually includes some reference to Venice, but there's evidence he was born in Padua and moved to Venice as a child. His signature may simply have indicated his association with the Venetian school of painting. Even the safe bet that some time between birth and death Angelo lived in Venice has been challenged by one art historian's claim that Angelo's adult life was spent in Turin. He may have abandoned city life altogether; there was a plague in Italy during his lifetime, and young men who liked to have their portraits painted fled the cities to avoid it. Homosexuals claim Angelo as their own, and certainly history shows no trace of a wife.

Luckily for the Harrington—crucially for it—an art historian at the University of Bologna had devoted her life to reconstructing his life on this foundation of lacunae, her masonry the handful of available facts, her runny mortar a mixture of gossip and guess. Before Gloria Scipi took up the cause there had been no books on Angelo, but over the course of five centuries he did come up from time to time. He had been mentioned in an eighteenth-century diary—writing of Angelo's *Portrait of a Gentleman with Leopard and Lamb*, its author, an Englishman on the grand tour, remarked on "an extravagant, almost garish portrait by an unknown painter that nevertheless stirs the sentiments in profound and unusual ways." An undated photograph of a painting thought to be a copy of a now-lost Angelo turned up at a Paris flea market, showing a young man gripping the head of his sword while three ringless hands, the gender of which cannot be determined from the photograph, reach blindly from behind a maroon curtain. A feminist art historian in the 1970s cited the prettiness of Angelo's noblemen as evidence of his destabilization of gender roles. In the 1980s various Queer Studies personnel, taking androgyny for homosexuality as Renaissance viewers themselves likely did, hoped that Angelo's bold work would inspire resistance to the queer-unfriendly Reagan Administration.

Many of the paintings themselves had been effaced— five-hundred-year-old paint smothered by century-old paint, inscriptions on hats and rings abraded and illegible.

Gloria Scipi did not let the absence of hard verifiable data deter her; on the contrary, it empowered her to set straight what little record there was and to make up the rest. Her monograph on Angelo, *Angelo Veneto: Painter of the Soul*, has a tone of weary authority and nonchalant erudition varnished by the glamour of discovery. She dutifully summarizes the few lesser efforts—so-and-so's hypothesis that Angelo worked in Brescia, so-and-so's claim that he was homosexual—and dismisses them all. She was responsible for identifying as Angelo's work the portrait of a gentleman with a razor-sharp pen that for centuries had been misattributed to Giorgione. Two of the chapters of her book were written as detective stories. In one scene she troops through a field in Fiesole to track down the landscape seen through the little arched window of the misattributed *Portrait of a Very Young Gentleman*, a landscape that Giorgione could never have seen but that Angelo knew intimately, though he never depicted it in another painting. There is no uncertainty in *Angelo Veneto: Painter of the Soul*, just Gloria Scipi bearing the truth.

It had occurred to Jon that maybe it was a poor translation that made the book, important as it was, seem so ridiculous. He had wanted to give Gloria Scipi the benefit of the doubt. But now, sitting at his little desk in his nonoffice with her catalog essay, he took it back. No translation could be this bad without some help from the original.

Adger had never liked the essay to begin with, and not just because it was so hard to follow. Gloria Scipi, the world's leading (and only) expert on Angelo, was never going to produce anything other than a scholarly introduction to the portraits of the great little-known cinquecento painter Angelo Veneto. Adger could edit it by making the Collection's *Gentleman with a Red Cape* seem as important as *The Last Supper*. In a foreword to the catalog he could go on and on about this being the painter's first one-man show; he could remind readers that it was being mounted not in Italy or New York but right here, in Atlanta, Georgia's, finest little museum. He could make his joke: there's hope for us all! But he could never expect Gloria Scipi's catalog essay to easily support the kind of high-concept blockbuster he wanted. He could never have asked her for that; she had too much dignity. And he had too much respect for her.

He gave the dirty work to Jon, instructing him to edit Gloria Scipi's catalog essay so that it made Angelo "come alive for the average person." Adger wanted to see her discussion of the Harrington's own Angelo, the hunk with the red cape, on page one of the final version of her essay, though it didn't appear until page three of the original.

Here is how that discussion began:

> In the *Portrait of a Gentleman with a Red Cape* (1515) in the Harrington Collection of Atlanta, this insouciance becomes a brutal male disdain for an unseen person who besides can only be a stand-in for the painter and, by turn, the viewer himself. Gone is Angelo's lighthearted and surface approach to the male gaze from the first decade of the century. We have penetrated the flesh to find the soul that lies beneath. This will to interiority that manifests itself in Giorgione more often than not as sentimentality, becomes in the Atlanta portrait something deeper and more shocking. *Soul* is the best

word here, despite the grave error of intellectual slippage committed by Jacques Moutard in his unjustly revered essay on the late quattrocento and the early cinquecento, *L'Âme et l'esprit de l'age.* The concept of the soul—in Italian, *anima*—could only exist in a religious context at this time, whereas Moutard sees it more generally as meaning "personality" and "interiority" without doing the necessary intellectual work to make the leap. Although its subject is secular, the overt religious context of the Atlanta portrait is clear. This gentleman's codpiece is crossed by a crease, a thin black line in the white fabric. This is the cross; the spread attitude of the gentleman's arms gives us the Christ, hanging.

Gloria Scipi was actually not all that bad. For instance, she went on to discuss with great authority a few other appearances around this time of the unusual scarlet color of the gentleman's cape, proving that the Harrington's portrait had been misdated by a decade. This was not news—she made this discovery years ago. The date she had assigned to the painting was the one that now appeared on the wall beside it. And yet the personal story she recounted—Gloria Scipi hot on the heels of the color red—still riveted.

Nonetheless—what was he going to do with this dog's breakfast! Jon had a self-immolating fantasy of opening the essay, as instructed, with the discussion of the Collection's portrait. Unaltered and unintroduced. The Christ, hanging.

Adger Boatwright waited for a cab to take him to the airport. He was going to Houston with a very young man. *(Beat.)* Giorgione's *Portrait of a Boy.* This was the joke currently being inflicted on the Ladies, as Jon knew from sitting outside his office all day. The Parmann Museum of Art was putting on a show of Renaissance portraits—*Every Face Tells a Story*—and Adger was the courier for the Giorgione in the Collection. Three blissful days without his boss—Jon would have time to brood and think, he would have space, he would figure this thing out.

The door to Adger's office was open a crack, and through it Jon could see him at the mirror, an early-nineteenth-century dressing glass of mahogany and white pine supposedly rescued from the ancestral plantation as it burned. Adger straightening his tie, licking his fingers and rubbing them all over his hair, checking his breath with his hand, trying out various faces. Jon knew that before any social engagement his boss also wrote out questions he might be asked, and the answers to them, on little scraps of paper that he stuffed into his pockets.

Adger emerged and leaned on the half wall, his big white head perfectly eclipsing the fluorescent light. His tie was crooked and blond curls shot out at strange angles around his ears. He reached down and said, "Shake my hand."

"Why?"

"Come on, shake my hand, be a team player, for Christ's sake."

Jon took Adger's big white moist hand, with its clear-polished nails, in his own.

"Come on, shake!" Adger said, squeezing.

"I am."

"That's how you shake hands?" Adger asked. "Just kind of flopping it up against somebody's hand like that, like it's being beached there? Why didn't I know that? I must have shaken hands with you in the interview, didn't I?"

"Uh—"

"I mean nobody wants to shake a hand that they think is dead, do they?"

"I think it's pretty obvious my hand is alive."

"Well, you better start showing some conviction if you want to be sure of that."

"Next time I will," Jon said, wanting to turn back to his computer screen.

"So what'd you think of mine?" Adger sheepishly asked.

"Your what?"

"My handshake. Do you think it showed conviction? But at the same time it wasn't too macho and bullying, was it?"

Jon smiled. Unlike the Ladies, he was immune to Adger's charm. But he could be moved by his insecurity, how much rehearsing he did before walking out onto the stage of life. "You'll be fine."

Adger reached over and snatched up Gloria Scipi's essay from Jon's desk. This was another good thing about his boss. The moment you began to have any troubling human feelings for him, he did something maddening to get you immediately over them.

Jon sighed as Adger shuffled pages.

"How is this coming along?" Adger asked, removing a jeweled fountain pen from his pocket.

"It makes no sense."

"Well, I know that, that's what I asked you to do—make sense of it."

"I'm trying, but first I have to understand what she's saying."

"Understand, understand." Adger was turning pages and scribbling. "This isn't the fucking Ivy League. Just do it!"

Jon snatched the pages back. The words "seminal masterpiece" now modified the title *Portrait of a Gentleman with a Red Cape* wherever it appeared.

"Don't look at me that way," Adger said. "Lighten up!"

"Go, Adger. Go to Houston."

"At least give me a title," Adger implored.

"For the essay? It came with one. 'Angelo—"

"Not for the essay. The show."

"Well, once I figure out what the show's about, I'm sure a title will fall into place."

"*Fall into place?* You mean like a silkworm falling out of a mulberry tree and onto your head? Think! You need to come up with the title first. Why do you think anyone goes to a show anyway? No one's ever heard of Angelo Veneto, you have to sell him. Do you know how I came up with the title *A Picture Is Worth a Thousand Words?*"

"Came up with?"

"It came to me in a dream. And here's something else. I gave the Parmann the title for their show." He was speaking in a whisper now, though there was no one else around. Beyond Adger's window evening sunlight fell through the branches of the oak. "I was having a drink with Elle MacArthur at last year's Biennale and it just came out. We were getting *very* cozy, if you know what I mean." Jon didn't blink. "*Every Face Tells a Story.* I told her she could have it."

"That was big of you."

"And I don't regret it. What benefits one benefits us all."

"I'll remember that."

"I have no regrets."

Adger's voice seemed to come drifting across a canal, you could hear the water moving in its masonry walls. But when he opened his mouth again the ghostly whisper, tinged with sadness, was gone. "I want a high-concept title by the time I get back," he barked. "I want you to do what I hired you for and put together a fucking *show*."

Jon was eating a bowl of cereal in the dark, staring at the *Portrait of a Gentleman in a Red Cape* projected against his living-room wall. He had stared too long. The painting had broken down into lurid patches of color; he couldn't get them to cohere. He couldn't get his life to cohere either. The challenges of his job were not the only problem. Atlanta was also a problem. If you had to leave New York for the South, you should at least expect consolation from the landscape—magnolia trees, plantation houses, squares with statues of soldiers pointing their weapons north. That would be interesting. But Atlanta had turned out to be a city of suburbs and ring roads. People drove forty minutes for a bagel. For Asian fusion, an hour. In front of every restaurant a squadron of crewcut boys stood waiting to pounce on your car. Jon saw all this but still didn't despair. He went to the Margaret Mitchell house and asked where the South was. The house itself, with its veranda and white columns, was promising. But the old docent inside shook her head and reminded him that Atlanta had burned in the Civil War—"the woe-uh," she had called it. He was genuinely sorry about this.

A key turned in the door. He was genuinely sorry about that too. He had moved to Atlanta with a man he was no longer in love with.

Ali came in, put down his shopping bag, and walked over to the couch. Jon's hand reached up and Ali took it.

"Shoo, what a basket," Ali said, staring at the wall.

Shoo. He had attended an English elementary school in Guyana, where he was taught to say "shoo" instead of "shit," "Hollywood" instead of "hell," as well as baroque ways to insult, including "You, sir, are a pest and a parasite." (What *that* was supposed to mean, Jon had no idea.)

"That's a noncanonical way of reading a painting," Jon sniffed.

Ali sighed, then in a chipper voice said, "I don't know about that, but I do know this is a gay painting."

This was something about Ali—the more miserable and

hostile Jon was, the more chipper and sweet Ali became. In anybody else Jon would have considered such relentless good humor passive-aggressive. But Ali was as guileless as a bowl of sherbet. Jon had seen this from the start.

They had met in a West Village bar when Jon was two years from finishing up in New Haven. He had come down to the City to see the Morris Louis show at the Modern, and in Jon's memory these two events became a single exhilaration. Experiencing the speed of the paintings, the rush of air around the poured stripes of color, led naturally to looking into Ali's face for the first time. His open expression, the great unpainted spaces at the center of the canvases. When Ali's face was at rest, his huge dark eyes narrowed as if about to close in sleep, the way a tall person might slouch to avoid calling attention to his height. Ali's embarrassed smile also seemed like an apology— he was too good-looking. He was the descendant of indentured Indians and Africans with pricetags; you couldn't help reading his glowing face as a narrative of the spirit triumphing over its enslavement! The long lashes, round face, cherub lips made him as beautiful as a baby. But his square chin was manly and jutted out, and throughout the day he had a five o'clock shadow that he covered craftily with foundation just lighter than his skin.

They had nothing in common, but they were young and soon living together in New York, and it had all been enough.

"A gay painting," Jon grumbled. "What could that possibly mean?"

Ali, unflappable, explained. "I mean, it's basically a painting that a man made of a big dick, except you can't see it, which makes it even sexier."

"Okay."

"Plus he's got a very pretty face."

"That's true, but I can't exactly put that in the catalog."

"It's so obvious. In fact, I don't think that's a painting of a man at all. He looks like a woman to me, packing a sock or something. What do they call them, drag kings?"

Jon took back his hand and Ali left the room. "I'm starving," he called from the bedroom. "Maybe I'll make us a curry. Does that sound okay?"

Jon turned to the figure in the red cape, who stared back. His eyes were rolled back into the left sides of their sockets, so that he seemed to be looking at you while keeping an eye on something just to your right. What was it? Jon walked up to the wall. A portrait of a woman in drag, a drag king—Christ, would he have to listen to this kind of twaddle the rest of his life? He stared deeply into the man's face. Jon was looking for the courage to leave. But he found something else: the man had no Adam's apple.

This was an observation that had never been made, or at least never recorded. That didn't, however, make it a good one. Unless you believed that every young gentleman living in the region between Venice, Ferrara, and Milan in the first decades of the sixteenth century was a total knockout, you wouldn't consider Angelo Veneto a realist. These are idealized portraits, they make their subjects look good. The guy in this painting has no Adam's apple, but he also lacks warts, moles, wrinkles, enlarged pores, hairs in his nostrils or along his ears. Angelo's innovation was working within the constraints of the new genre of the bourgeois portrait and still managing to convey something unseen and, if not unflattering, then disturbingly complex.

Jon projected another image on the wall. The *Portrait of a Gentleman with a Sword*, soon on its way from Rome, shows a green-eyed young man with a gaze directed somewhere to the left of the viewer. Again, no Adam's apple. Wisps of brown fuzz collect under the guy's chin, pointing toward the bright white column of his neck, which sits at the very center of the painting. His face is lit at an angle, the right side in shadow; the neck, under the overhanging jaw, should certainly be shadowed as well. Was Angelo, a faultless technician, deliberately calling attention to the fact that his subject had no Adam's apple?

One after the other the portraits vanished from the wall and were replaced. Some of the figures confronted you, others dismissed your very existence by looking away. But every subject was painted from the same angle and held his well-lit neck up for your inspection.

"I got some cauliflower at the market." Ali had changed into shorts and a tank top. His limbs were long and lean, his build boyish. He was pursued by men and women, he had been propositioned by straight couples and gay ones, money had been offered twice. His popularity soared once they moved to Atlanta, where no one had ever seen anything like him before. And still he remained humble and true.

"Gosh," Ali said, "I haven't seen you smile in weeks."

"Oh, come on." Jon called up the *Portrait of a Gentleman with a Red Cape*, then said to the wall, "I'm sure I must have smiled by accident every now and then."

"Not really."

"Well, no wonder Adger keeps telling me to lighten up."

"How is he, is he still pudgy and cute?"

"He's still a closet case and a lunatic. Now, here, come sit down and look at this with me. What you said about this being a woman—was that a joke?"

"How am I supposed to know?"

"Look closely." Ali sat down alongside him. "None of these guys has an Adam's apple. And you can't tell from the clothes because they wear so many of them. This one has at least four layers on—there could easily be breasts under there, right?"

"It's just a painting," Ali pointed out.

"Okay, right, but you were the one who suggested there might be more going on here, so that's what I'm trying to find out."

"I better start defrosting that chicken breast."

"Just wait. What do you say about the stubble on his chin?"

"I don't know. It looks like someone who doesn't really need to shave yet."

Jon turned to him and nodded. Then he called up the next painting, the *Portrait of a Youth in Green Velvet*.

"We were selling a vest like that last season," Ali said.

This, amazingly, was not a non sequitur. "To women, right?"

Ali nodded. "I guess everything comes back in fashion if you wait long enough."

"This guy has a full beard," Jon said. "So how can he be a woman?"

"That's a fake beard," Ali pointed out with the certainty of Gloria Scipi.

Jon went up to the wall and examined the patches of colored light. "How can you tell?"

"He's probably too young to even grow a full beard like that." Ali walked up to the wall and pointed to the subject's ear. "Also there's this little line going back here over the ear that looks like a string to me. Too bad we can't see the other side of his head—he probably had another one holding it up there."

"Oh, my God," Jon said. "I thought that was a strand of hair."

"It's a totally different color. His hair is dirty blond and the string is somewhere in the burnt ash family. Now, if I don't eat something—" Ali said and walked away.

"Can I use this?" Jon asked. "I mean, I'll give you full credit for everything, but can I use this for my show?"

"I don't mind," Ali called from the kitchen.

———

They ate Ali's delicious curry and drank a bottle of wine and then went to bed. It had never been hard for Jon to conjure the old feelings. He remembered seeing Ali for the first time, sleeping with him for the first time, walking down their block of the East Village with bags of flowers and food. He could remember being in love. But it had been a long time since he felt it.

At first it didn't matter that they had so little in common. Jon was happy to have things to prove—that a Jew and a Muslim could fall in love, that an art historian and a ladies sportswear salesman could enjoy each other's company year in and out, that love could transcend all. But Jon found he had a sentimental attachment to Israel; Ali considered religious states scary. Ladies sportswear did nothing for Jon; Ali found papal patronage dry. And as for Love—it could transcend everything but a move to Georgia. Jon didn't love Ali enough for that. But now, watching Ali sleep, listening to him swallow the cooled air, each inhalation a little gasp, so that he could as easily have been in a state of constant amazement—Jon felt he was wrong. He had been so stressed out about his job that there hadn't been room for anything else. Now, lightened of his burden, possessed instead of possibly the greatest insight in the history of Angelo scholarship, Jon once again felt his great love for Ali. Who cared that their c.v.'s didn't overlap?

Jon closed his eyes and watched the darkness gently turn.

The critics—the feminists, the homosexuals—had been on to something. But they never quite got there. Once you accept that the subjects of Angelo's portraits are women, things more or less add up. You have an answer to questions. Why do these figures stare at you so fiercely? Why do they threaten you with a weapon, if it isn't the most dangerous and disruptive mystery, the mystery of gender, that they're challenging you to solve?

The layers of fancy-patterned clothes and rich fabrics and feathered caps were men's fashions of the times, but what dandy dared pose with nosegays, with ribbons and ring cases and birds? Why all the phallic props, the bulging bright codpieces?

These are portraits of women not disguised as men but instead masquerading as them. You aren't supposed to be fooled. The string that Ali pointed out running over the left ear of the guy with the green vest—look closely and you see the faintest trace of the line continuing across the top of his forehead. Jon was sure that infrared would show what could only be a headband, raising the possibility that this was originally a portrait of a woman. What might have been a woman's diadem was here a band holding up a beard, which itself becomes, once you know how to look at it, totally fake, the Groucho Marx look of the cinquecento.

You understand these things. And you understand why Angelo's subjects have never been identified—none of them, ever, unlike Leonardo's or Bellini's or Dürer's, unlike those of his contemporaries Lorenzo Lotto and Andrea Solario. Angelo's portraits never reveal his sitters' identities, despite their clutter of accessories and props, despite the specificity of the background landscapes. Only the Louvre's *Portrait of a Boy with a Hammer* dares include a name, on a little scroll curled at the subject's feet, a motif echoed by the sneering curl of his lower lip, as if the scroll is something he's cast aside or is about to step on. The name is Martino, nothing else, and Gloria Scipi, after producing a list of seventeen Martinos known to have lived in Venice at the time, throws up her hands and hedges her bets by pointing out that a *martino pescatore* is a kingfisher, symbol of industry and steadfastness, and that its breast is the same color as the arrogant boy's cap.

Understandably, she preferred to discuss Angelo's work and life in the context of the new kind of portraiture being produced in the first half of the cinquecento. She focused on what could be known and made up what could not. But she didn't use what little evidence she found to invent identities for Angelo's sitters. She scarcely acknowledged that these identities were in question. And she never asked this: how could all of Angelo's subjects have remained unknown for so long? These are not archetypes. These faces are not the male equivalent of the *bella donna*; they do not include Christ, despite the religious connotations that Gloria Scipi found here and there. Indeed, if a single thesis could be plucked from the tangled garden of Gloria Scipi's scholarship, it was that Angelo Veneto invented a new kind of portrait by investing his subjects with specific psychologies (which she insisted on calling souls), thereby making them look like real people (albeit incredibly gorgeous ones). She ignored the absence of contracts or anything else that might have identified them. In her everyday work she gathered clues, she was hot on trails—but when faced with an obstacle she was more demolition expert than detective, and if she couldn't make a big bang, she didn't accept the job.

And so it fell to Jonathan Weitz to bestow upon the world the answer to a question that had not yet been posed: why is "Martino" sneering at his name?

An evening of discoveries, a night of love—at six the next morning Jon packed a bag. He was moving into the museum. The Harrington Collection was housed in a refurbished 1927 Coca-Cola bottling factory on a quiet stretch of Peachtree Street. Jon had never seen a peach tree on Peachtree Street or anywhere else in Atlanta—but that didn't matter to him anymore. The Old South may have been gone with the wind, but here was something new to seize his imagination. Except for the occasional minivan of private school students, nobody visited the Harrington Collection when there wasn't a show on.

Adger's zeal for the blockbuster exhibition made sense, and Jon had to admit that the execrable *Picture Is Worth a Thousand Words* was a stroke of marketing genius. The five paintings, like the rest of the Collection, went mostly unseen when they could be viewed for free, but gathered in a single gallery on the other side of a ticket taker, they had patrons lined up around the block. Of course after Jon's Angelo show opened, Adger's *Picture* queues would be remembered as a couple of folks who happened to wander in off the street. But until that day, or at least until Adger's return, he had the museum mostly to himself; he could sit on the floor in front of the *Portrait of a Gentleman with a Red Cape* undisturbed for hours. He could sit with his laptop and write; he could look up at the painting and see what could not be seen projected on a wall; he could close his eyes and fantasize about the brilliant curatorial future that would be his.

This was the plan. It was, he knew, ironic that the very morning after rediscovering his love for Ali he took a sabbatical from it. But Adger would be gone only three days and Jon had to make every second count. He had an essay to present to his boss on his return, a fucking show to put together. And what else would he be doing but developing Ali's revelation into something he could share, something they both could share with the world? What other muse could Jon possibly want?

Ali was still in bed. The white sheet was draped at a provocative slant around his waist, like the Venus de Milo; one of his eyes was open, the other squeezed shut. Jon rubbed the hair on his lover's tummy. Desire tugged. But Art called. "It'll be good, I'll finally be able to get this show together," he explained. The other eye opened. Jon pressed his lips against Ali's and said, "It's all right with you, baby, isn't it?"

Ali smiled sleepily and said he didn't mind.

———

The first thing Jon did when he got to his desk was reread Gloria Scipi's essay. He'd been through it a dozen times; he'd even read it in the original Italian twice, though he didn't know the language. He'd been willing to do whatever it took to fix the essay. But now, reading it in light of what he, alone of all art historians, knew, he saw the answer quite clearly—the essay would have to be jettisoned and replaced. Gloria Scipi didn't just assume these were portraits of men; her analyses of the paintings rested on this premise. Her use of the term "male gaze" to describe the intimidating stare of Angelo's subjects referred not to a certain way of looking but indeed to a man. Her very focus was on the manliness of Angelo's subjects; her claim that the gentleman with the red cape was a Christ figure, for example, was supported by the cross she saw in his codpiece.

Jon set the essay aside and went downstairs with his laptop. He sat before the *Portrait of a Gentleman with a Red Cape* and wrote.

He started with a formal analysis. Later he would develop an argument, stitch observations together into a narrative, provide a historical context, fill in blanks. He didn't have much time but he didn't panic. He wasn't in graduate school, he wasn't obliged to ascend to the ethereal realm of theory—he could ignore the transcendental signified, stop trying to recall the concept of the decentered gaze. He wasn't after difficulty; his goal was comprehensibility, transparency, the lifting of veils. If he shone a light on the paintings, if he helped viewers see them as they were intended, then he would have done his job.

He barely ate. There was no café in the museum and no decent food within a fifteen-minute drive. The secretary, a nice lady with pewter-colored curls, brought him in a piece of a mayonnaise caramel cake she had invented and unselfconsciously named after herself, and when he told her how much he enjoyed "Delia's cake," she brought in an entire quarter. He made coffee at the sink when he was tired; he slept, when he had to, in a sleeping bag under his desk. The rest of the time he sat like a supplicant beneath the painting. When his back could no longer be appeased by stretching he sat up against the wall on the other side of the gallery, under a Giorgione; he still had a clear view.

The publications specialist took advantage of Jon's availability to remind him repeatedly of deadlines. She was a pert young blonde who carried around spreadsheets warning that the catalog wouldn't be ready for the opening if he didn't hurry up. He smiled at her and nodded. He had someone more formidable to answer to, and it wasn't even Adger.

The few visitors—mainly rich-looking women, thankfully none of the Ladies themselves—smiled down on him. On the first day he was asked if it was a school project he was working on. Of course he would be mistaken for a student—he was dressed in shorts and a T-shirt, and sitting on the floor. On the second day he was asked if he was an artist himself. He had a day's worth of stubble now, it was a bad hair day—he supposed he looked like an artist, a twenty-first-century one, sketching with software. On the third day—still thankfully not the weekend—visitors navigated wider circles around him or looked to the guard for explanation.

Changes may have been observable on the outside, but they were nothing compared to what was happening inside him. What socioeconomic circumstances could have coalesced to produce these transvestite pictures that their subjects couldn't have commissioned, that were destined to hang behind closed doors for one hushed century after another—this was for Gloria Scipi, not Jonathan Weitz, to explain. He knew only what he saw. The painting was full of playful little deceits but what they added up to wasn't playful at all. Its subject's taunting arrogance, her self-satisfied smile, her menacing stick—it's obvious she has a secret. And so what happened to the person who figured it out?

Visions apparently took place at lesser museums than the Louvre. But instead of a room full of Renaissance guys jostling for Adger Boatwright's attention, it was one person, a young woman with fair hair tucked into a red cap and little breasts hidden behind a great red cape, who stepped out of a painting and moved toward its startled viewer, Jonathan Weitz, associate curator of Atlanta's Harrington Collection, the first person in centuries who understood. He felt a seizing up just below his chest. He was in that altered state he had hoped for but never attained, as hard as he tried—fasting and swaying those Yom Kippurs of his childhood, he had only ended up starving and faint, once even passing out on the altar, with the Torah in his arms. In college he abandoned religion for art. And still he waited.

Jon exhaled, his body relaxed, he was jelly quivering on the floor.

"Why don't you go on home?" a voice said.

Funny, it didn't sound like the woman from the painting. And it was coming from somewhere else. Up and to his right. There was something casting a shadow on his feet. His head turned toward the sound.

"If I had a beautiful boyfriend like that waiting for me at home, do you think I'd be here?"

It was Dinitia Sims, the security guard. You cannot move into a museum without an ally, and she seemed to like him. This had everything to do with Ali. He had come to visit Jon at the Harrington shortly after Jon started there, and Dinitia hadn't stopped talking about him since. On his way up to the offices Ali had stopped to introduce himself. He had scarcely been to a museum before Jon met him; maybe he thought talking to the security guard was something you did. If Dinitia liked Jon, it was because he had the good taste to have Ali as a partner.

Jon smiled. Words were forming slowly in his brain.

"I mean, y'all are still together, aren't y'all?" she asked.

He nodded. "He's great. I'm going to see him tomorrow, don't worry."

She seemed relieved. "Out of the two of y'all, who the one cooks?"

He wondered if she was asking who the woman was in their relationship. "He does."

She nodded knowingly. "Was it his mama that taught him?"

"Yeah." He was here in this room talking to this person, he got it now. "When we lived in New York we used to eat over there all the time. She makes the most amazing West Indian food."

"Did she teach him how to make pepper pot? Does he cook you *bacalao*?"

"Both," he admitted. "And he makes his own hot sauce."

"Damn. And what do you do for him?"

"Sometimes I cook."

"Oh yeah? What do you fix him?"

She had his number, there was no way spaghetti or scrambled eggs would convince. "Saltwater soup," he conceded. "A porridge of bitter ash."

"That sounds nasty," she said, shaking her head.

"I mean I used to."

He didn't have time for this. Adger would be back tomorrow. Jon had been staring at the painting during the day and writing through the night and still he wasn't finished.

"I have to get back," he said.

But as he spoke, something terrible occurred to him: *What if he was wrong?* He had staked his entire professional future on this insight, which suddenly seemed a possible derangement. Dinitia would say nothing but still Adger would discover Jon had been camping out in the museum. Adger must already have known something was up—Jon hadn't answered the phone or responded to any of his boss's messages, which he was leaving more and more frequently. Jon was counting on the ends justifying the means. But what if the ends amounted to nothing more than the end?

There was probably no one in the world who had looked at the *Portrait of a Gentleman with a Red Cape* more than Dinitia Sims had.

She was on her way back to her post when Jon said, "Wait. Can I ask you something?" She turned around. He took a deep breath. "Have you ever noticed anything funny about this painting?"

"Funny?" she scowled.

He nodded and waited. He didn't want to ask leading questions.

"That's a good-looking white boy, that's all I know."

"White *boy*?"

"Yeah."

"Could it be a woman?" he blurted.

"Could be," she said. "Never occurred to me."

Could be!

"No, it never occurred to me," she went on. "But if I was going out looking like that, you know I'd tote a stick along with me too."

Adger was leaning against Jon's ledge. He had had some kind of sunscreen issues in Houston—red blobs swam like goldfish across the broad bowl of his face. "I admit I considered it," he was saying, to no one in particular. "I talked to Elle and she said I should have known not to hire someone from the Ivy League in the first place. She hired one as a male secretary once and he refused to type."

Jon smiled. He saw no need to remind Adger that he hadn't refused to type. The evidence, all fifty pages, was sitting in his chair. Adger had just got in from the airport and apparently hadn't seen the essay. He sounded wounded by Jon's silence, betrayed. He was making it known that sparks had flown from his head in Houston and now he was contemplating something grave. Jon, meanwhile, was in a state of quiet well-being, serenaded as he was by the unheard music of his own freshly minted words.

"At least he answered the phone," Adger went on. "What were you thinking!"

Jon smiled. "I was thinking about art."

Adger looked down at him suspiciously, then went on. "She said I should let you go. I would have listened to her too. I wanted to give her *something*. I mean it became clear pretty early on that I didn't feel the same way about her as she did about me. I don't know why women are always trying to change you."

It wasn't believable that Elle MacArthur, director of one of the foremost small art museums in the country, had embarked on the unsophisticated project of trying to change a gay man, closeted or not, into a straight one. Adger must have been talking about some other change. He seemed to be considering something. There was a strange pleading look in his pale blue eyes. His right hand rose to his mouth, a manicured nail darted toward his lips—vestigial nasty habit, whiff of candied fruits—before dropping out of sight on the other side of the wall.

"I would have listened to her except I decided to give you one last chance and try your home phone. I figured you might be *working from home*," Adger sneered. "So I called and talked to Ahmed."

"Ali."

"Did he tell you I called?"

Jon nodded. Ali was the only person besides Dinitia he had spoken to in three days. Jon had called home twice, and always Ali sounded fine and wished him good luck in getting his work done.

"We had a nice chat," Adger said.

"Did he tell you about—" But the question was pointless. Of course Ali had said nothing.

"Did he tell me about what?"

"Did he tell you he handed me the thesis for the catalog essay that's sitting on your chair?"

"Thesis," Adger said, frowning.

"Just read it. Don't worry."

"That sounded more convincing coming from Ali. He told me not to worry too. Said you were working and"—he made quotation marks in air—"'mustn't be disturbed.'"

Jon rushed to his boyfriend's defense. "They taught him how to speak that way in school."

"Well, they did a good job. These days everybody talks like they come from the ghetto, have you noticed?"

Random sentences from Jon's essay read themselves to him. This was the best way to put it—it wasn't his own voice he heard. Adger sounded far away and Jon had to strain to hear him. Jon leaned forward and cocked his head. Finally, he stood and leaned against the wall behind his desk, trying to muster an attentive look.

Adger didn't seem to notice anything unusual. He was staring at the framed poster for the *Picture Is Worth a Thousand Words* show just to the left of Jon's head. But it was badly lit, and Adger could only be looking at his own reflection.

"An Arab and a Jew together," Adger said. "What y'all are after I can't imagine, unless it's the Nobel Peace Prize."

It went without saying that Jon had no interest in explaining to his boss what an Arab was. Still, Jon's ordeal at the museum had somehow changed him. Art, it seemed, could make you a more patient person, if not a better one. He walked around his desk, leaving the protected waters of his cubicle for the seaward channel controlled by Adger Boatwright. But it was Adger who looked panicked. When Jon's hand reached out his boss flinched. But he didn't budge. The hand reached up and up, its fingers finally making a gentle landing on Adger's unevenly broiled cheek.

"Does it hurt?" Jon asked.

Jon returned to his desk and tried to work—there were a hundred things he had been neglecting. Instead he stared at Adger's door and waited. But when the door finally opened three hours later and Adger came out smiling, it was anticlimactic— not because Jon knew Adger would like his essay but because it no longer mattered to him if he did.

"Listen to this part," Adger said, staring down at the page. Jon sat there as Adger read aloud, deliberately, presenting Jon's own essay to him, making sure he got it:

> Despite Leonardo's groundbreaking portrait the *Ginevra de' Benci*, which legitimated the three-quarters view and the head-on stare (rather than the profile) for portraits of married women, respectable women at the time Angelo was working generally did not meet men's eyes. The belligerent stares of Angelo's *travestite* shift our focus from the very fact that these women are gazing at us. Because the undisputed "male gaze" at work here belongs to the artist and by extension the viewer, the glares

of Angelo's subjects subvert the convention that women should be looking away in paintings or in life. Angelo, progressive as he was, could not bring himself to paint these women *dressed as women* and glaring this way. The models themselves may not have felt comfortable with such audaciousness; it was easier to put on a man's cape and pick up a stick than stare out at a man from under a diadem and a great pile of curled hair. Only through the radical practice of drag could the artist and his subjects make the more radical point that women are not demure possessions, that they are *self-*possessed. In the *Portrait of a Gentleman with a Red Cape* Gloria Scipi has found "something deeper and more shocking" than anything in Giorgione. Scipi interprets this something as "soul" and sees this as a religious painting, a representation of a soul; contemporary viewers are more likely to see the painting as an early representation of the workings of the modern mind. Whichever interpretation one accepts, it must be complicated by the fact that Angelo located this inner core in women dressed as men. Soul and mind are hidden away in the body just as these women are hidden in men's clothes, but our inner selves can be revealed by the strong artist's hand.

That this artist is male blah blah blah . . .

"Of course it's going to have to be completely rewritten," Adger added.

"It is?" Maybe Jon wasn't completely indifferent.

"It's too academic. You aren't at Yale anymore. No normal Southern person thinks drag is a radical practice. I'm not even sure what that means."

Jon wrote this down.

"And do you know what this reminded me of? Those Calvin Klein models, those androgynous ones—they're always pouting. There's just *so* much you can do with this."

Jon nodded.

"And what about Madonna, where she wears a suit in that one video?"

He nodded again.

"Why do you keep nodding, you're making me nervous—I feel like you're agreeing with me."

"I am. If you want to know something they do at Yale, writing essays about Madonna videos and Calvin Klein ads is it. If you want to connect it to Angelo—"

"*I* don't want to connect it but everyone who comes to this show will." This was pure Adger—he was the opposite of a populist but he wanted to be popular. "Nobody knows anything about Angelo Veneto, I've told you that before. Consider your audience—what do you think I did in *A Picture Is Worth a Thousand Words*? You need to give them something familiar to jump off of. Forget all the theory about drag. Leave that to the queers. Or write an essay yourself and publish it in *October*. Frankly, my dear, I don't give a damn!"

He had misread Adger's smile. But Jon wasn't being entirely ingenuous when he asked, "Is there anything you'd keep in that passage?"

"Obviously these gals in drag themselves, that's what's going to bring in the hordes. And this:"—he looked up from the page and solemnly quoted—"'Our inner selves can be revealed by the strong artist's hand.'"

"You like that?" Jon beamed.

"I do, and you probably have no idea why. That's why I'm having this conversation with you." Jon waited and Adger continued. "You want to help people relate to the pictures. What do people care about more than their own inner selves?"

Jon had no answer for this. If he thought of himself as Matthew Arnold, keeping a steady eye on the object, then Adger Boatwright was unabashedly Walter Pater, the grandiloquent Victorian appreciator who said that "the first step towards seeing one's object as it really is, is to know one's impression as it really is." What was looking at art, for Adger, but figuring out how it makes you feel? *A Picture Is Worth a Thousand Words* had included a room full of computers, each displaying a blank page bordered all around with a black line. In this frame visitors were encouraged to type in their own "thousand words, or hundred words, or however many words you feel like writing!" Would-be critics were instructed to take inspiration from the five paintings in the exhibition and give their imaginations free rein. When they were done they clicked Submit and their however-many-words were projected into one of the empty rococo frames alongside reproductions of the masterpieces themselves. Adger didn't seem to care that soon visitors were spending more time looking at these examples of fin-de-siècle free association, uninformed and un-spell-checked, than at the great paintings of Western Civilization themselves.

Jon had of course been appalled. But was Adger's idea, then and now, really so wrong? He'd quoted Jon's own essay to illustrate his Paterian perspective, words that to Jon sounded no less dulcet than anything else there. To discover the work of art as it truly is—this seemed to be the very task Angelo set out for the viewer with his gender-bending, am-I-or-am-I-not paintings. But do his subjects say, *Look at me closely and tell me what I am*? Or do they say, *Look at me closely and tell me how I make you feel*? Or simply, *Look at me closely and feel*?

In the end, it was only by submitting to these paintings—something he had avoided, even dreaded—that Jon was truly able to see them.

"Also," Adger said, "I like the behind-the-scenes stuff about what the models were thinking."

"That was kind of speculative," Jon allowed.

"Keep it!" Adger bellowed. "People are fascinated by models. And we're still going to have to figure out what to do with Gloria's essay. She'll have my fat white ass on a stick if we don't use it. We'll have two catalog essays. What's wrong with that?"

"Just give me your notes and I'll rewrite my essay." Jon reached up and grabbed hold of a few pages.

"And here's something else." Adger wouldn't let go of the pages, no matter how hard Jon tugged. "This part about the *Ginevra de' Benci*? Let's replace that with the *Mona Lisa*. Everyone knows the *Mona Lisa*."

"Uh, okay, but the *Mona Lisa* comes after the *Ginevra*. The *Mona Lisa* can't be a forerunner to Angelo because it's contemporary with his early stuff."

"Well, there's a great connection between two great painters!"

Jon smiled. His hand dropped. "Sure, Adger, I'll work in the *Mona Lisa* somehow."

Again and again light flooded the foyer of the Harrington, and when it was all over, several images of Adger Boatwright in the center of a kick line of Amazonian drag queens had presumably been captured for posterity. A photographer from *Time* had been dispatched to the opening of *Drag Kings: Angelo Veneto and the Mystery of Gender* to illustrate an upcoming cover story that was certain to incense much of its readership and make the Harrington Collection nationally famous.

Jon stood watching over the photographer's shoulder. He had stared into the paintings and when he looked up he saw this—a museum full of drag queens. It seemed, alarmingly, like cause and effect. Of course the opening was all Adger's doing. The supposed countercultural phenomenon of drag kings may even have been his invention; drag *queens* were easy to mobilize but the drag *kings* he had managed to produce, three clear-skinned young women, had slicked-back hair and shoe-polish sideburns and minimal interest in sustaining a male persona, much less the illusion of being men. Jon was innocent of kings and queens, and the only time he ever glanced at a national newsmagazine was at his shrink's office. He was responsible only for the show's scholarship. In the end he'd omitted Madonna from the catalog essay, left out Calvin Klein, and Adger didn't seem to notice or care, but still, why deny it, none of this would be happening if Jon hadn't made his bold claim.

Adger had arrived on the arm of one of the Ladies, and it didn't matter that since then she had busied herself elsewhere in the museum, advising wannabes with checkbooks on how to become Ladies. To watch Adger making like a Rockette with towering transvestites was to see a man convinced of the inviolability of his closet. He seemed unaware that when the photograph appeared in *Time*, the pale chunky blond in the center would be universally assumed to be homosexual. He had become as secure as his old tormentors from Claxton High. This was a great event, and no one could possibly think anything funny was going on.

Jon had one of those moments of wistful affection for his boss that punctuated his general exasperation with him. Ever since Adger had given the thumbs-up on the transvestite angle, these moments had become more frequent, starting to seem less like punctuation than like the relationship itself—dashes got longer, periods piled up and turned into ellipses, great gaps in which Jon felt Adger was actually a pretty decent guy. Once, Adger invited him into his office, something he'd never done, and the two of them sat together at Adger's desk—a pecanwood door, supported by sawhorses, that had been rescued from the silkworm plantation and was believably charred at one end. Jon's arm had rubbed against Adger's, and Jon felt a rush of hot blood.

Jon snapped out of it when the photographer asked everyone to form a conga line. Jon went to find Ali, who had gone to get drinks. The bar was on the other side of the crowded main gallery and Jon plunged in. Connoisseurs and critics turned away from the paintings and toward one another, pretending not to notice two CNN anchors, a man and a woman, who had shown up together—a double surprise, for nobody knew they were a couple, and they were dressed in black, a color they were contractually prohibited from wearing on air. Jon pressed through. Several drag queens had gone for a severe bohemian look and these had not been asked to pose for *Time*. They stood there exchanging furious barbs and didn't notice Jon as he maneuvered past them. He ran into the museum director, who did not mar his perfect record of silence toward Jon but did nod at him, an acknowledgment of his existence and, Jon believed, his achievement.

When Jon was near the bar one of the three Ladies standing in front of the *Portrait of a Very Young Gentleman* caught his eye and waved. He pointed to the bar but she gestured for him to come to her. The Ladies were dressed in taffeta ballgowns, in wraps and pearls and diamond tiaras. Wonderfully, the one who beckoned with a tan bony finger was wearing a crimson cape, a duplicate of the one worn by the catalog cover model, the gentleman in the red cape.

"I told my husband, I said, 'Honey, we've been duped!'" she was saying as Jon approached. She grabbed his arm and held him there. Kisses flew but the conversation continued.

"And what'd he say?" another asked.

"He said, if it'd make his hourly rate go up, he'd go drag too!"

"I'd enjoy seeing your husband in a dress," the third remarked.

The second one seemed scandalized but the first, wife of the husband in question, did not. "Funny you should say that," she said, "because I declare, I think he *liked* the idea of a woman dressed as a man."

"Honestly," the second one said, "there's nothing *radical* about a woman wearing pants. I don't see what all the fuss is about."

"You mean in the paintings?" the third one asked.

"It's not the clothes per se," the first lady explained, "it's just that gals didn't dress that way back then."

"These ones here could very well have been common whores," the third one said.

The second lady raised an eyebrow but the first chose to ignore this remark. "Do y'all know what I think about sometimes? There was no reason on God's green earth why someone like Leonardo da Vinci couldn't have painted two colored rectangles on canvas the way Mark Rothko did."

"He had the talent," the second one confirmed.

"Well, exactly," the first one said. "But there was just something keeping him from doing that. Or what about painting a canvas black? Could Leonardo da Vinci have physically picked up his brush and painted a canvas solid black? I'm fascinated by that."

The third, taking her revenge on the first for letting the subject of whores drop, said, "For goodness' sake, why don't we ask Jon. I mean, he did go to Yale." She turned to him. "What do you think, dear?"

"Jonathan Weitz," the first lady, undaunted, said, "you haven't said a word to us all evening."

He smiled apologetically, then said, "I think I know what you mean—that whole narrative of quote-unquote progress in the history of painting is just so overdetermined."

The Ladies stared at him.

"With what you figured out," the second one finally said, "you should be the belle of the ball tonight."

"Actually," Jon said, pointing toward the bar, "my boyfriend should be."

The Ladies turned.

"He was the one who noticed these were paintings of women," Jon said.

The third lady put on her glasses. "I recognize that boy. He sold me the cutest top. It had a sequined Stars and Bars on it. It was a hot top."

Jon grinned and the second lady turned back to him. "Well, I had no idea."

The first lady glared at her, then politely asked, "How long have y'all been friends?"

"Not long enough," Jon replied, and the Ladies smiled an uncomfortable smile.

Ali had reached the front of the line at the bar. He was wearing a black suit with white frills coming out of the arms and neck. The barman, a pretty Filipino in a green bellman's outfit, said something to Ali, whose shy embarrassed smile stretched from ear to ear, his face full of light as he turned away and stared at the floor. That smile seemed to buoy him over the crowd, above the catty queens and rivalrous Ladies, the posers and pretenders.

"Hey, baby," Jon said, kissing him on the ear.

"Hey!" Ali said, as if he were surprised to see him here.

They took their drinks and stood flanking the *Portrait of a Youth in Green Velvet*. "This party is fabulous," Ali said. "I just saw Chad Rockman a minute ago."

"He was standing in front of the Milan portrait," Jon said, "with Estelle Dulaney."

"I know, I can't believe it. I wonder when they see each other—they're in totally different timeslots."

Jon stuck his nose against the back of Ali's neck and inhaled his citrusy cologne. Ali, a good sport, tolerated it for a while. "Wait till we get home," he finally said.

"Are you ready?" Jon asked.

Adger appeared with a wild look in his eye and a gin and tonic in his hand. "Hey," he said, sticking out the other hand in Ali's direction. "There's the man with the eye."

"Oh, please." Ali held his drink up in the direction of the hand. "I think I have an eye for fashion, but that's about it."

"You were working at a boutique in Buckhead when I met you at the Christmas party," Adger said.

"Yeah, and I was telling Jon"—Ali gestured with his drink to the painting—"we were selling a vest like that just last season."

Jon turned in Adger's direction and smiled apologetically —a reflex.

Adger's sensibilities, however, did not seem offended. "I'll have to come visit."

"I had no idea you were into ladies clothing," Ali said.

"What, didn't you see me up there with those drag queens? Your *friend* did." He turned to Jon. "Because I could see you standing there smirking when they were taking a picture of me."

Interesting—Adger had posed with drag queens for what he believed to be a portrait of himself.

"I know that look," Ali said.

"I wasn't smirking," said Jon, feeling very ganged up on. "I was smiling. That's going to be a cute picture."

"Jon disapproves of all this," Adger informed Ali. "Well, I say what's wrong with getting people into the museum? Get the drag queens in here, bring them on! Angelo would have loved this party."

"I don't disapprove," Jon said. Were we, he wondered, always found out?

"It's all right, you're a big shot now," Adger said. "You can get any job you want in academia, you're cut out for that."

"I can?" Jon asked. "I am?"

"Here's something they don't teach you in the academy," Adger declared. "If there ain't no money for the gold leaf, there ain't gonna be no halo round the Virgin's head!" He broke into song: "Money makes the world go around, the world go around, the world—"

"Jon hates retail," Ali put in.

"That's ironic," Adger let slip.

"We were just leaving," Jon said.

But not quite yet. A tall thin creature in crocodile pumps and belted black minidress strode toward them, her hair a medusa's black coils, her face a carved mask of fury. Classical, but in Prada.

The blood rushed out of Adger's flushed face but he soon recovered. "Gloria!" he cried. His arms shot out, as if he were doing calisthenics or pointing out emergency exits. He kissed her on one cheek and was heading toward the other when she pushed him away. Regaining his footing, he said, "What an unexpected honor you've graced us with!"

"Why unexpected? I have the invitation." She reached into her enormous black purse and held it up for Adger's inspection, then let it drop. It was printed on good stock and fell straight to the floor. "For what you invited me I do not know."

"Why we invited you! You, Gloria Scipi, the number one scholar of Angelo Veneto in the world! You are the guest of honor. I just wished you'd called us and let us handle your arrangements." He wagged a finger. "I don't want to be hearing now that you're staying at the No-Tell Motel."

"I make my own arrangements. I was not going to come. I decided finally to come for one reason."

"And we're so fortunate and honored you did," Adger said. "Isn't this marvelous?" he added, gesturing to the walls.

"Menzogne," Gloria Scipi spat. "Perfidia. Tradimento."

"Prego!" Adger cried.

"Who is Jonathan Weitz?" she demanded, pronouncing it *Vites*.

"Allow me to introduce him," Adger said with delight. Apparently, Jon's job description included taking heat. "Signora Scipi, this is my assistant, Jonathan Weitz. I think he did such marvelous work with the catalog, don't you? And this is his friend, Ali."

"You look fabulous," Ali said, but Gloria Scipi made no sign of hearing.

She and Jon sized each other up. She started at his shoes (scuffed, from Macy's) and worked her way up. He kept his gaze fixed on her fierce face; he was frightened but had enough presence of mind not to be the first to look away. He'd never met her; they hadn't exchanged email or spoken by phone. Adger had said he'd "handle" Gloria's essay, by salvaging the biographical sketch of Angelo and the survey of the scholarship, and Jon happily turned it over. When Jon finished his own essay, it was Adger who sent it to Gloria, presumably with "Ciao Bella!" and some florid pidgin Italian equivalent of "FYI" scribbled across the front page. Weeks passed, and Adger and Jon had both been relieved when they heard nothing back.

"I want that you understand what you have done," she said.

Jon's heart leapt into his throat but he managed to say, "It's an honor to meet you, Professor Scipi."

He didn't realize he had extended a hand until she took it and began leading him away. Her hand was hot. He glanced over his shoulder at Ali, who was saying something to Adger.

Gloria Scipi and Jon stopped in front of the *Portrait of a Gentleman in a Red Cape*. She smelled of hyacinth powder and new leather and a recent cigarette. Their arms were so close, he could feel them straining toward each other. They shared the same space before the painting, their essays were side by side in the catalog. Couldn't their critical positions be reconciled? He had opened a door wide enough for the juggernaut Gloria Scipi to charge through. He would gladly let her! But Gloria Scipi wasn't going through that door. She stared at the Angelo, her eyes filled with tears.

"This," she said, "is a man. A real man."

The subject of the painting looked like such a ponce in his red velvet cape that Jon was tempted to make a joke. *Real men don't wear red capes!* Instead he said, "Yes, I know that's the canonical interpretation and—"

"This is not an interpretation!" she cried.

Jon wished it could be their two essays having this conversation. In writing he was articulate and sometimes elegant; in person, neither, never.

Like Milton's Satan, like Jon's mother, Gloria Scipi could see the chink in the armor and wasn't afraid to needle it. "Say it," she said. "Look at this painting and tell me your thesis, say it so that I can hear it, so that we can all hear it, *a voce alta!*"

"Professor Scipi," Jon pleaded, "this is just my interpretation and—"

"Do you go to the psychiatrist?" she asked.

"I beg your pardon?"

"Do you?"

He didn't see what this had to do with anything, but what could he do but, miserably, answer? "I do, I go to a psychiatrist."

"And do you tell him your *interpretations* of your symptoms?"

"It's a she, and as a matter of fact I do."

"And how does *she* respond?"

For the first time since Gloria Scipi appeared Jon felt like laughing, though under these circumstances he couldn't even smile. "She's never impressed, no matter how clever I think they are. But I keep trying."

"Do not bother. You will never impress this woman of intelligence and you will never be cured. And do you know why?"

"— —"

"She is not interested in your clever theories, because interpretation is not the point."

"Maybe not in therapy," Jon conceded, "but—"

"Not in anything! Interpretation kills!" Gloria Scipi turned back to the painting and said, sadly, "You killed this painting. You killed Angelo."

Upstairs, Jon sat at his desk in the dark. His hands out of habit came to rest on his keyboard, but they were trembling.

His instinct was to try to pass the blame back to Adger, who had so gleefully passed it on to him. Had he been seduced by Adger's tabloid vision of the museum, his shameless appeal to the public's baser instincts as a way of drawing them in? Had it all been a temporary aberration, the product of which Jon could disown, as if this were just a way to make money that anyone would understand and excuse, one of those degrading jobs that you take as a young person and that confer an odd dignity on you when you recount them in your memoirs, like pole-dancing in Reno or writing for the *National Enquirer*?

No, his catalog essay was passionate, and he believed every word. The world had only the paintings as evidence. Gloria Scipi looked at them and saw men; Jon looked and saw women. So sue him!

I want that you understand what you have done.

Jon had turned the five Angelo portraits into a show. This was what he had done. He had allowed himself neither the time nor the luxury to dream about the rewards of his work before Gloria Scipi materialized in Atlanta to demonstrate the costs. She publicly attacked him and would no doubt lead the assault against him in print; she had the power to destroy him in various arenas, he supposed. But these costs were small change compared to what he had had to do to the art to get the show to cohere. Jon hadn't killed Angelo, he hadn't even killed the paintings, as *la profesora*, that drama queen, had charged. Jon hadn't even explained them away. But with his revelation he had opened the door to more scholars with more explanations. The paintings would survive this crush or they would not. He hoped they would.

Jon needed to go home, but the only way out was through the gallery. From up here the white noise of the party was almost soothing, the way the ocean at night can sound if you aren't in it. But the only person who could lead him safely between Scylla and Charybdis—Adger Boatwright and Gloria Scipi—was Ali. Where was he? Ali would console him. He would take him away from all this.

A sound came from Adger's office. Jon stepped out of his cubicle. Adger's door was closed and there was no light coming through the crack underneath. Something fell, the impact muffled by the Persian rug—a small object, maybe a book. Whispers ensued. Jon pressed his ear to the door and held his breath. He could hear cars speeding down Peachtree below Adger's window, he could hear the party below. Adger's office by comparison was not just quiet but free of sound.

"You are so exotic," Jon heard Adger say, finally. "You turn me on!"

"I thought you were just interested in me for my idea," Ali teased. "I mean, it was no big deal. I just noticed they were women."

"Shh, shh," Adger said.

"I mean, hello, what man would wear a green velvet tunic like that, unless he was a drag queen," Ali said. He always got very talky when he was drinking.

"It was the Renaissance," Adger snapped. "That's what men wore. Now shut up and give me a little sugar."

"I don't care if it was the Renaissance or whatever," Ali said, giggling but adamant. "Those aren't men, they're women."

"Well, you don't have to convince *me*," Adger said. "I don't give a damn."

"You mean you don't think they're women?" Ali asked.

Again that terrible, total quiet.

"I think we sold it, that's what I think," Adger finally said. "And a good time was had by all. Now shut up or I'll shut you up with this. You're prettier than a striped snake and you're turning out to be double the trouble."

"Don't say 'Shut up,'" Ali giggled. "Say 'Show some silence, sir.'"

"*Shh*," Adger said, "I think I hear something."

The door cracked open, the weather balloon of Adger's head squeezed out. Jon pitched forward. Adger screamed. He tried to shut the door but Jon's legs were in the way—now it was Jon crying out as the door slammed into him again and again. When the door swung free of his legs he shot forward, then crawled to relative safety under Adger's coatrack. *Did they have coatracks on plantations?* was the dangerously irrelevant thought that came into Jon's head. Adger loomed over him. Jon squirmed away and rolled against the wall, rubbing his throbbing shins.

Adger stood by the closed door with his head bent, his long arms hanging straight down, pulled by the weight of his clasped hands. A streetlamp rose in a window across the room, a sickly pinkish-yellow light slanted in, casting a nimbus around a figure on top of Adger's desk. Its face was dark and featureless but it appeared to be naked, all thin limbs and sharp angles, and just above the level of the desk, something jutted out—Jon and Gloria Scipi could easily agree on the gender of this one. He could have been modeling for a portrait or carved from stone. He must have sat in perfect stillness and perfect arousal as all hell broke loose on the other side of the room, and he continued to sit this way as Jon and Adger caught their breath.

Jon's eyes adjusted to the darkness. The look in his lover's doe eyes was a little sad but didn't waver, and Jon understood he had not seen more than he was meant to see.

Fire Year

I

The town sprang up at the intersection of roads leading to the district center and to the city. It was a region of lakes, banked with soft carpets of grass in summer, covered with crystalline ice in winter. But from the start, when the king granted its charter, the town was a rude place, with a plain wooden church and an assembly hall and an alehouse around a square, with pestilential ditches and muddy lanes. The townspeople were craftsmen and merchants, they traded anything they could make or grow in the dirt behind their houses. There were Jews in this town, and the king granted them the right to work and to build their own house of worship, as long as it wasn't as tall as the church. The Jews made a living and survived periodic slaughters and lived their lives mostly unchanged as war came and went. The area already divided into quadrants was further divided among three kingdoms, with districts and counties and even cities split in two, along natural borders like rivers and unnatural, invisible lines. But the town remained whole. The kingdom became the dukedom and then the dukedom ended, and the Jews multiplied until they were the town's most numerous inhabitants.

Twenty years after it was built, the synagogue burned down. Seven years later a fire swept through the town and seven years after that another fire blazed. The town's actual age continued to appear in official histories, but for the Jews the destruction of the synagogue became year zero. Even a century later the fires continued to return, and in those years the town, with its modest houses clustered around the market square, knew once again the suffering it had in the quiet years forgotten. It was a town full of numerologists, they counted things obsessively, and not just years—and to count they used letters as well as numbers, for every letter corresponded to a number, and so words of more than one letter were not just words but also sums. The number seven and the seventh letter of the alphabet, while unavoidable, could at least be used sparingly, so as not to tempt fate.

Rabbi Aryeh led no congregation and had no formal training in Talmudic studies—but he had a group of devoted students. He preemptively pointed out to his fellow numerologists, many of them his elders, that it was tempting fate *not* to use the letter *zayin* in names, and that if the Lord so blessed a family with seven sons and the mother of these sons was tired, then may she be entitled to a little rest! (At the time of this remark Reb Aryeh had only one son himself and didn't seem to acknowledge or even notice the misfortune of having so small a family.) And so it came as a shock but not such a surprise when he did what no one in living memory had done: to his second son born in a seventh year, he gave the name Zev.

His wife, Rokhl, was delighted with this slap in the face of superstition. She understood without ever having discussed it with her husband just what his choice of name meant. She herself had fallen under suspicion two years earlier for parading her firstborn baby, Isaac, in the market square. She left his face uncovered despite his blue-eyed beauty, thereby affront-

ing the townspeople with her lack of fear of the evil eye, a lack
that seemed to stand for some greater and more threatening
one that nobody, out of respect for her husband, dared even
think. For her part she felt that the presence of such beauty in
that rotten mouth of a town should be made known, so as to
increase the general happiness; and she was proud of him. The
townspeople avoided looking at the baby when they greeted
the rabbi's wife in the square—but the subject was never discussed, and so she never had to defend herself. Two years later
Reb Aryeh had to defend his own affront only once, when Reb
Shimon, head of a rival school and of the Society for Morality
in the Young, appeared at Reb Aryeh's schoolroom door and
asked if the prohibition against using the letter *zayin* in the
name of a male child born in a seventh year, whether this prohibition that perhaps, for who knew God's mind, was responsible for the new synagogue never having burned again and for
the town never having burned down to the ground, whether
this prohibition was now declared over.

"The new synagogue is made of stone," Reb Aryeh pointed
out, then invited Reb Shimon to come in.

They sat across the long scarred table from each other. Reb
Shimon looked around. It was a rougher room than his own
school, it certainly didn't look like the site of a teaching phenomenon. He could not imagine it packed to the rafters with
students, though he knew Reb Aryeh got more than his share
of students, and not just from the town but from as far away as
the district center, where they had their own, superior schools.
But of course it had nothing to do with the room and everything to do with Reb Aryeh, whose every word his students
took as holy. *The new synagogue is made of stone*—was this an
example of Reb Aryeh's famous wisdom?

Reb Shimon had come hoping for Reb Aryeh to admit his
error or at least clarify his position, explain how much weight

it was meant to carry. The entire town was waiting for guidance from this strange man. Reb Shimon had no illusions about the task at hand. For despite the town's long-standing bias against sevens, the number was, as everyone knew, the luckiest of all. He had expected Reb Aryeh to bring this up, perhaps not even bothering to cite the Midrash: "All sevens are beloved." Reb Aryeh might simply have moved on to the more obscure Talmudic recipe to combat tertian fever that began, "Take seven prickles from seven palm trees, seven chips from seven beams, seven nails from seven bridges . . ." Like a good chess player Reb Shimon made no move without knowing how his opponent would respond, and he had an answer prepared for each citation Reb Aryeh might bring up. But Reb Aryeh (who, despite Reb Shimon's suspicions, was as wedded to numbers in his daily life as any of the town's other numerologists) did not talk about numbers at all.

"The town already has a lion," Reb Aryeh said, referring to his own name, Aryeh. "Why not a wolf as well?" he added, referring to Zev's.

"Reb Aryeh," Reb Shimon said. "There are reasons behind traditions. In this case, the reason is so that the town will be spared from fire."

"But even with entire classes free of Zevs and Zaks, classes full of misnamed Josephs and Aris and Moishes, it is still God's will that the town burn."

"Not lately!" Reb Shimon said. "We haven't had a fire in a seventh year in decades."

In fact it had been nearly half a century since the seven-year cycle had been regular, the fire coming six years after its predecessor, then eight years, then seven, then five, then four, then nine.

"You see?" Reb Aryeh said. "Perhaps God has freed the number seven of its curse."

"Reb Aryeh," Reb Shimon said, "I do not need to remind you that even in irregular times such as these, the fire returns every seven years *on average*."

"And so how is a fire in a sixth year any less terrible than a fire in a seventh?" Reb Aryeh asked impatiently.

Reb Shimon had no answer for this. Instead he asked, "Do you see the town still standing?"

"Reb Shimon," Reb Aryeh said, "the town burns because we make fires in our homes and most of them are made of wood and still have straw roofs. For this reason the fire will return periodically like a beggar to whom you've given charity once, even if we give our sons the names of fish. Don't worry, nothing will change."

Reb Shimon felt a little sad, as he always did when someone he knew gave up a habit, even a bad one. What next, he wondered, what next? The second synagogue had been called the new synagogue for a hundred years, Reb Shimon suddenly realized, the modern-sounding Aryeh himself having used the word "new." But the second synagogue wasn't new at all! If anyone other than Reb Shimon himself realized this, would they all then be obliged to start calling the synagogue something else?

"Don't worry," Reb Aryeh said again, this time sounding a little worried. "The sum represented by my younger son's name is nine, and in this regard the name could be considered safe."

In addition to Reb Shimon's Society for Morality in the Young, that town of three thousand Hebrew souls had a Society for the Dissemination of Russian Culture, a Society for the Dissemination of German Science, a Resettlement in the Holy Land Society, a Resettlement (Anywhere) Society, a Society for Talmud Study, a Society for Torah Study, a Society for the

Study of the Prophets, a Sickbed Society, a Burial Society, an Interest-Free Loan Society, and a Society for the Dissemination of Knowledge Among the Jews. Some of these societies were homegrown; others were funded by contributions from as far away as St. Petersburg. Out of the ashes of every fire rose a new society, as villages and capitals, as Jews and non-Jews, came to the town's aid, opening it up to money and new ideas. To the great numbers of these societies Reb Aryeh had added another one, the Society for the Prevention of Fires. It was only thirteen years old, founded in the aftermath of a fire with money from a reform-minded nobleman in a nearby village, and already the municipal decree that it had engendered was responsible for nearly two dozen brick homes. The decree banned the construction of wooden houses in the center of town. The Society raised the money and provided the manpower to fight fires and help householders rebuild. In this way the fires became less and less destructive.

Some of the townspeople worried that the brick homes were a way of taunting God, who could easily find another way to torment them as He saw fit. Perhaps even a worse way. To this Reb Aryeh said, "Nonsense. This is just being careful. On occasion," he conceded, "it's careful to heed a superstition, as the *Sefer Hasidim* states. But to believe in a superstition at the expense of your livelihood and even, God forbid, your life, this is not showing proper care for God's creation. We must stop the fires from destroying our town." The municipal council agreed. Rarely again was the concern raised, though as the years passed, the townspeople could not help noticing that the Society for the Prevention of Fires had not prevented any fires—they came and devoured what houses they could. And though it was commendable that the Society always seemed to have the money to help a ruined townsman rebuild with the mandated but more expensive brick, it was also suspicious, considering the numbers of houses that burned. Was there not also the possibility—the unspoken question arose—that people were burning down their own houses in order to receive one otherwise reserved for the rich? Evidently those who held such suspicions did not notice the barren places everywhere in the town center. Although nearly two dozen houses had been rebuilt in the last thirteen years, almost twice that number had been lost, many of their inhabitants having lost their lives along with their homes, many more having left that cursed town for good.

II

When Zev was seven years old the town burned. The towns-people hadn't foretold the season—it was the month of Sivan, when spring was giving way to summer—but no one was surprised by the year. Zev had been born in a seventh year but not a fire year—the town had burned the year before. The regularity of the fires had come to seem like a divine gift—forewarned, you could take precautions, like not naming your son so as to provoke. Once the pattern was broken, seven decades after the old synagogue burned, the townspeople saw they had no way to prepare. Although they were comforted that the cycle had righted itself—they knew the town would reliably burn again in seven years—they shunned the boy whose own father had so presumptuously made him an agent of history.

They shunned him out of fear but he gained no power from this, because he could not believe that he, a skinny timid boy, could possibly be the cause of this fear. He was left alone at the religious school he attended, even by the teacher, who returned his work without a word and with no mark but a perfect score, as if the teacher were afraid to touch the paper any more than necessary. In the town there were almost as many schools as societies, and indeed many of the societies were affiliated with schools, whose curricula reflected the primacy of their concerns. There was even a school, sponsored by the Society for Workers, that taught no religion at all. This was the school Zev's older brother, Isaac, attended. (He could have studied with Reb Aryeh, but he was not a scholar and anyone could tell he was not meant to be one, as his mother told his disappointed father, who finally conceded the point.) It was a rowdy place, with arguments settled by fistfights and, as Isaac recounted it, a recess ritual that involved a well-built boy named Josef, whose father was a coachman, standing in the field behind the school and silently daring the other boys to take him on. With horror and fascination Zev pictured the entire student body, the bravest on the front line, moving toward this Josef and then shrinking back at the least of his moves—a step taken forward, an arm raised.

At age fourteen Zev still enjoyed frightening himself in this way; it made him feel better about attending his father's school, where his classmates left him alone. He even liked imagining that this Josef would take him over his knee and break him in half. Surely this would feel good, or at least come as a relief, the way a piece of putty stretched to its limit wants nothing more than to snap. But this terrible pleasure seemed entirely out of reach. Josef, along with a couple of other boys he had chosen, made himself very present in the market square; one had no choice but to engage them or avoid the place entirely. These bullies knew Zev was Isaac's brother. Isaac was not one of the bullies, but he was one of the brave boys from the front line and as such had earned Josef's respect; sometimes Isaac even appeared with them in the square. Still, this was not why Zev could pass with nothing but the darts of their gazes on him—they too wanted to avoid contamination. But whenever he approached the square Zev's blood pulsed in his fingertips at the prospect of the rough handling he risked.

When he was not in school, studying, or reciting his morning, afternoon, or evening prayers, Zev ran to the lake nearest town. It was the smallest of the region and, perhaps as a result, had no name. Its banks were less grassy than those of the other lakes. Trees grew right up to the waterline. This lake was almost perfectly round and its water was freezing even in summer. It was reputed to have no bottom, for those who had stood in its rocky shallows just under the trees and then taken a single step out found they had no footing.

The nameless lake belonged to Zev. He couldn't swim. But he had a place to sit between trees and stare out at the water and try to engage in the silent meditation his father taught. It was either this or plunge into the freezing lake, for in this fire year, this year when everyone expected the town to burn— knew, feared, and half hoped it would—Zev himself was about to combust. The only question was when, though there was the faint yet definite terror that the answer might be never. But you could forget about all that, at least for a moment. You could forget about the seething of your body, you could forget about it all. You closed your eyes. Zev's father taught that you just had to close your eyes—and breathe. "It is God's spirit in your breath," Reb Aryeh would say. "Listen to yourself breathe. Breathe evenly, but not *clop clop clop* like a horse—let your breath flow like a stream. Let your head empty of words and picture yourself at the foot of the Divine Throne. It isn't covered in rich velvet, nor is it threaded with gold—and yet what a beautiful sight! A throne made entirely of light." Zev closed his eyes and saw the throne. It was beautiful—but always about to vanish. He breathed in, he breathed out. He tended to breathe with such determination that more than once in class his father had told him to stop trying so hard.

It was the start of summer. The surface of the lake shone. Overhead a great spider's web stretched from one tree to the next. This was the last thing Zev saw before closing his eyes, and he continued to see it in his mind's eye. The web was beaded with rain from a morning downpour, and in the midday sun, in that single ray that penetrated the dark forest, the web appeared jeweled. A comforting illusion. In fact Zev knew the world to be a web of evil you had to break out of. No, this was too easy, this good-versus-evil business, this child's way of thinking his father would openly have mocked. Better: the world was a web of passions, each stitched to the next; you could be trapped in the web or be master of it. *Web* was not a word his father ever used to refer to the world, it was Zev's own metaphor, and though he recognized the meagerness of this contribution to his father's thought, he thought the image made sense. This was the universe and this was man's choice, to be the fly or the spider, to sit coiled in death or to swing across the damp and sticky surface of the world.

Zev was still the fly, a dirty little fly! No—he had simply not yet mastered his passions. Every night, in the room he shared with Isaac, he pretended to sleep until the moon reached a certain height. What light streamed down through the pear tree and the milky glass was barely enough to see his brother lying alongside him, on top of the sheets. But Zev's imagination furnished what his eyes could not. In the meager light he held his breath and saw that the world was flooded with radiance.

And so why in the true light of day did this divine gift seem like a test of biblical proportions, one infinitely more difficult than any he had taken in school?

Zev breathed in and out, too fast, too conscious. His father was right—he tried too hard. But his case was more urgent than most. When he opened his eyes again, it was as though his other senses had opened as well, and only now did he realize the damp of the forest floor had soaked into the seat of his pants.

III

When the ancient sage Reb Yaakov died, a lengthy will was found in his briefcase. In this document he ordered all ten men of the Burial Society to go to the mikvah before handling his body. Reb Yaakov had been a scolding teacher and a joyless leader of his congregation. The rants of his sermons became more intolerable as he aged, and his congregants began awaiting the day when he could finally find peace. It took much longer than anyone had thought, and when the day finally arrived, the entire town made sure his last wishes were honored to the letter, so that his spirit should remain carefree in God's presence and never have cause to return.

On the day of the funeral the ten men left their houses and fell into a procession down the town's central road, toward the bathhouse. This sight moved Zev to ask his father to explain. Everyone knew the men would have to bathe after handling the body—why were they washing themselves before? Reb Aryeh replied that it was Reb Yaakov's day to teach, not his. Later the ten men escorted Reb Yaakov's body, itself purified and wrapped in a sheet, through the town and to the graveyard. The body was so small that the four men who held it seemed more than was necessary. If he hadn't known it was Reb Yaakov, Zev would have thought a child was being taken to the pit.

The next day Reb Aryeh told his students that Reb Yaakov ordered the men of the Burial Society to go to the mikvah in case any one of them had recently had a nocturnal emission. Each was required to immerse himself 310 times, which was why they emerged from the bathhouse so long after entering it. Reb Yaakov was adding his voice to a discussion that had been taking place for centuries. While spilling one's seed was a sin, its terrible consequences in the afterlife could be avoided by taking a bath.

The class listened in silence. Finally, the bravest student asked, "And how do you know whether you've had one?"

Most of the other students suppressed a laugh, but Zev continued to listen gravely.

"This is a good question," Reb Aryeh said. "Although the Talmud prohibits touching the penis for this or any other purpose, it acknowledges certain difficulties this prohibition might cause."

"But why did all ten have to go to the mikvah?" another student asked. "It's unknown whether even one of the men had had an emission the night before. Is it possible all ten did?"

"Do you really believe that this of all sins was what worried Reb Yaakov the most when he wrote his will?" Reb Aryeh replied. "Here is a man sitting at his desk thinking of his own end. Were the missed procreative possibilities of the men who would handle his body really what concerned him?"

The answer clearly was no, but no one dared utter it, since no one knew what to say next.

"Of course not," Reb Aryeh answered himself. "Reb Yaakov, may he rest in peace, was not just giving these men a chance to clean themselves. He was giving them a chance to look into their souls—this was his final blessing to them. It made no difference whether they sinned in the night or during the day. It made no difference what their sin was. He wanted them to repent. This is how we do so, as you already know—in a group. And so why do you worry about examining yourself with your hand? You should be worried about *not* examining what lies in your hearts and in your souls."

When Reb Aryeh brought them all to the mikvah the next Sabbath eve, Zev looked at his classmates differently. About himself he didn't have to wonder; he was a sapless tree, a dry well. But was it only to purify themselves before the Sabbath that *they* were there? He couldn't ask them this question. Day after day they looked through him as if he were a ghost, never addressing a word to him. Perhaps it was because he didn't exist for them that they didn't seem to fear contagion from stepping into the same water that he did. On the contrary, they laughed like children, giggled like girls. Zev could only imagine why.

He stepped into the tepid water and didn't stop until he was fully immersed. Crouched on the floor of the mikvah, his skinny body bare, a scum of stray hairs floating over his head, he felt like a king, clad in raiment of silk. That his father had led him to this pleasure of the senses was proof enough that the path of righteousness did not always diverge from the path of physical pleasure. Indeed that only through the body could righteousness be attained—the body made in God's image. What else did man in his puniness have to offer? What thing greater did he possess?

The lake Zev had never dared set foot in could not feel like this. He imagined it was colder, so cold it could stop the heart. It may have been just as holy as the mikvah—Reb Aryeh taught that the water needed to "live," to flow from a natural source—but to Zev's knowledge it had not been blessed. It was the presence of his brother's body in water that blessed it, and so Zev knew the mikvah had been consecrated. His father had brought him to the mikvah when he became a bar mitzvah. His brother had come too—this was a ritual Isaac actually enjoyed. After Zev came out of the water, he stood next to his father and watched as his brother descended. The perfect V rising from his waist, the compact muscles ranged between his shoulders— this was not a scholar's body, Zev thought, and he wondered if his father was thinking it too. It worried Zev that Isaac wasn't a scholar, for it meant his brother's future was unknown to him. The smooth white marble of Isaac's skin—if this was what Terah's idols looked like, no wonder Abraham had seen such power in them and smashed them all. As he descended, the straight black hair on his brother's legs floated up and pooled on the surface of the water, surprisingly long and fine.

IV

Zev had been born in the month of Elul, at the end of summer, and it had not gone unremarked that his birthday fell in the season during which the risk of fires was greatest. But now that it was almost fall, his fourteenth year had nearly passed and the town was still intact. After he turned fifteen, there would be only one month left before the new year, and if, God forbid, a fire came during this month, then certainly he could be said to have nothing to do with it. But even if God chose not to burn the town this year, Zev expected no great change in the attitudes of the townspeople toward him. He sensed they almost wanted their town to burn—or at least for the cycle to remain righted. They couldn't imagine a world free of fires. The best they could do was believe they could anticipate them, not even to control them but rather to be prepared, to confirm their ability to see the divine plan, feel more secure of their own place in it. Narrow, yes, ignorant, yes, they were even stupid. Isaac openly mocked them and the town itself. He dreamed of moving to the city, which he had never even seen; dreamed of going to America, *planned* on ending up there. And upon his confidence bordering on arrogance, the ignorance he mistook for certainty, Zev saw a shadow fall, and the shadow, he feared, was sin. Zev kept his thoughts to himself, though he hoped that if he could just attain his birthday without a fire, then maybe a change would come to other areas of his life as well.

The last month of Zev's fourteenth year was passing more slowly than the previous eleven months combined. It was as though time were stuck, and he himself stuck in it, although he was surrounded by evidence of time's passing. Even at its height the sun hung a little lower in the sky. Shadows, including his own, lengthened along the forest floor, and occasionally on the wind came the breath of the tomb. Afternoons buzzed like the undertone of a thousand voices, the days stretching themselves so taut that it seemed they would snap open, though the deluge that was always about to pour forth never came. Perhaps for this reason there was something new in the gazes that fell upon him, something at once imploring and threatening, as if the townspeople expected him to bring forth either rain or fire, or at least expected it to be in his power. Now when Zev fled to the lake he looked over his shoulder, worried he was being followed. This made it that much harder to concentrate when he closed his eyes and breathed and waited for something to happen.

The nights were still hot, but this didn't bother Zev, who barely slept anyway. It was in the small hours of the morning when he felt most calm. Isaac turned from side to side and even after he had fallen asleep continued to turn, trying in vain to find a cool spot. He tangled himself in the bedclothes he had cast off to begin with. This frenzy of activity made it more perilous for Zev to stare. Although he was in a position to know better, he imagined that Isaac regularly had the fabled nocturnal emissions, his seed as numerous as stars. Sometimes Zev thought he saw Isaac's eye opening, and Zev closed his own eyes and stiffened like a corpse regardless of what position he happened to be lying in. Sometimes he shifted his gaze to the door.

Isaac had once conjured a golem there. Zev was nine years old. When the moonlight struck the back of the door so as to illuminate it fully, Isaac had Zev stare into the glow until the door seemed to vibrate, and out of the light itself materialized the golem, taller than a man, greenish of hue, an emissary from the world of darkness. This was how Isaac described it during that year of trying to scare his brother to death. Zev saw how maddening it was to his brother that he wasn't scared, that in his fascination with the game and with the attention he seemed incapable of fear. And so Zev played along. He saw the golem, he did, but it took form from his brother's words rather than from moonlight. He tried to appear scared—*Oh!* he cried, ducking under the blanket. Isaac's hands reached under and grabbed him, the deep voice crying, *The golem is going to get you! The golem's hands have gotten you! The golem will take you away down below!* Zev lay there screaming with his heart pounding and his eyes closed, hoping the golem would keep him in his clutches as long as it took to reach the Promised Land.

Now Isaac ignored him like everyone else in town; not to avoid contagion but simply because Zev had no place in his brother's life. Zev was too young to be one of the boys Isaac passed his free time with in the market square. He would always be too young.

The only time they spent alone together and awake was when they walked silently to their father's schoolroom to attend the nighttime readings and then walked back home. As Reb Aryeh's son Isaac couldn't avoid the readings. Reb Aryeh's students roused themselves every morning at half past midnight. They read from Lamentations, remembered the destruction of the Temple in Jerusalem, beat their breasts. They cried together, Zev more loudly than the rest. He pulled out strands of hair, pounded the thin bones of his chest until they ached.

Surely he wept the bitterest tears. And yet through his blurred vision he clearly saw Isaac sitting there stony-faced, thinking of something else.

V

Reb Aryeh taught his students the law through the perspective of the emotions—those that needed to be controlled and those that needed to be expressed. There were fourteen in all. Humility he placed high on the list; also love. The town had never known this kind of teaching. The rabbi's knowledge of the emotions seemed so intimate that he must have experienced them all, even the sinful ones. The townspeople whispered about him, even as they sent their sons to his school. Reb Aryeh explained to his students that by knowing themselves, by always moving toward ethical perfection, they would also move closer to God.

The range of man's emotions was great, but it seemed to Zev that in the schoolroom during the day his father talked about nothing but lust. "When you feel the Serpent of lust coiled around your heel," Reb Aryeh instructed, "stand barefoot on a cold stone floor." It didn't even matter if you happened to be married, for sexual relations in marriage were also strictly regulated. You were commanded to make love to your wife on the usual occasions—holidays, on the eve of the Sabbath, before a departure and after a return—but also whenever her own passions were stirred for you, this point seeming to set Reb Aryeh apart from the town's other teachers, their cold dry gazes almost as blind to men's passions as they were to women's.

And yet Zev knew that his father's advice, however well intentioned, was wrong. Zev would never dare say it, it was probably a sin to think it—but standing on a cold floor only cooled the feet, it did nothing to douse the flames of the loins. Certainly, it didn't clear the mind. Zev knew because he had tried. He stood on freezing stone and turned his gaze to the wall—and thought of his brother. His father once told about the man in synagogue who closed his eyes to say the *sh'ma* and saw a beautiful woman. There she was, in the darkness behind the man's lids—and the only way he could make her go away was to open his eyes. But to do so was not to say the *sh'ma*, not to call out to the people and with the people that the Lord was one. To open his eyes was to cut himself off from God and man.

Even though his age was a matter of public obsession and only at his peril did he lose track of it, Zev couldn't remember how old he was when he heard this tale. He couldn't remember it well at all, for it had meant nothing to him at the time. The story may have been set on the Sabbath, or perhaps it had been a holiday or just an ordinary day of the week. But the urgency of the man's plight Zev remembered. Also Reb Aryeh's solution: keep your eyes closed, and in this way you will remain in God's presence.

Perhaps if Zev could rest he wouldn't worry so much—but it was the worry that kept him alert, prevented him from sleeping to begin with.

His brother did not have this problem. Even when he was tossing about he was fast asleep; his ears were closed to his own sonorous snores. Their father never so much as looked at Zev in class, though more than once he caught Reb Aryeh stealing amused and only mildly exasperated glances at Isaac during the midnight readings, Isaac who was never more than half awake; his sleepy eyes contributed to his charm. Zev couldn't blame his father, though he expected more from such a great sage, an attitude other than the moonstruck one everyone else had around his brother.

There were times when you had to wake up.

Every night Isaac had a hard time getting out of bed for the midnight readings. Zev had always encouraged his brother gently, tickling his toe, trying to pull his arm out of its socket—the kind of thing a younger brother feels entitled to do. But one night, when Isaac would not budge, Zev jumped into action. He felt a kind of energy pulsing through him, he was, despite the season, shivering. In an act of ventriloquism that startled him, Zev said, "I know what you're feeling, that headache you have from being roused from a deep sleep. But don't succumb. Be swift like a raven, don't think, just stand up as if you're only a body responding to an impulse, then wash your hands, as prescribed by law. Also wash your face, even though there's no requirement to do so. I find that helps me wake up. If you do this just a few times in a row, instead of lying in bed for another few moments as you always do, then you've developed a good new habit. It gets easier, I assure you. The deed is easier than the thought—try it, you'll see!"

Isaac looked at his younger brother blackly. Getting up never got easier, as Zev himself could see. "Tell him I'm tired." Not *Father*; not even *Papa*—but *him*. "I helped Mama in the market all day. I'm too tired to do anything but sleep. It's not normal to be awake at night anyway."

"But we do it every night!"

"Night is for sleeping. For God's sake, even an idiot could tell you that. I bet it's in the Torah."

"Don't take God's name in vain," Zev said.

"Why not? I don't believe in him anyway."

Zev gasped, and all the air was sucked out of the room.

He had been fearing for his brother's soul for a long time, but now Zev's sense that it was in imminent peril was confirmed. It wasn't that Isaac was too tired tonight to go to the midnight reading. It wasn't, as he seemed to be saying, that he was too tired *every* night. The reason he was never really present at the readings was because he didn't believe in God. He wasn't just slipping beyond his family's reach; he was in danger of slipping beyond the reach of God Himself.

Had Isaac gone back to sleep? Zev looked into the future and what he saw wasn't good. And so, abandoning theology, he leapt on Isaac's back, pounding it with both fists until his brother relented and got up.

After the readings, when everyone else had gone back to bed, Reb Aryeh began to write, opening the books that served as barricade during his classes. He wrote every day but the Sabbath, although nobody had ever seen a word he had written. He used no notes in class or in his public lectures; he had never published a book.

Zev came from behind him one night but his father didn't notice. Zev apologized for disturbing him. His father turned around, interested to see what his son had to say. "Father," he said. "It's about Isaac. I want to tell you something. To help him." Zev tried not to notice the spark in his father's eyes at the mention of Isaac's name. "He told me something," Zev forced himself to go on. "He told me, he, God forbid, doesn't believe in God." Reb Aryeh cocked his head, then shook it, and Zev, watching closely to see if he was nodding yes or no, could not finally decide. Whatever his father was doing, he didn't look surprised. "Aha," Reb Aryeh said, "you make him sound like one of them." "Father?" Zev asked. "One of them," he repeated. "His opposites. Those who live by the law and die by it and never talk to themselves in between. Do you think they who know everything but believe in nothing believe in God?" Zev had never thought of this; he felt derailed. "You can follow the letter of the law without believing in God, obviously. They only believe in God who believe in perfecting themselves morally to be worthy of God." "But Isaac—" Zev feebly began before his father cut him off. "Why should Isaac say he believes in God if he doesn't? When he's ready to believe in himself, then he'll be ready to believe in God." "But he's always late to the midnight readings, and I thought it maybe was because—" "It's maybe because he's comfortable in his bed that he's late. You of all people know he's got a comfortable bed, doesn't he? Do you think I want to get out of bed?" "But you do it." "Of course I do. And he will too, eventually. If he isn't so perfect, it just means there is something left for him to learn."

VI

To control anger, Reb Aryeh advocated a method that to Zev sounded as dubious as standing on a cold floor to overcome lust: "Think of a friend lying on the battlefield with a sword stuck out of his neck and blood spouting from his throat."

Instantly, Reb Aryeh could see the enjoyment on his students' faces as they thought of a friend—or an enemy or anyone at all—with a blood-spewing gash and a sword through his throat or with a knife in his back or with one or both of his eyes gouged out. Or with his genitals gored into pulp by a bull.

The rabbi could see these images pass across the students' faces, and before any one of them could open his mouth to make an idol out of his teaching, he said, "Now, what kind of advice is this? Why is imagining such a horror a good way to control anger?"

"It gives you perspective," said one student. "How important is your anger when your friend is lying dying on a battlefield? You must rush to his side!"

"No," disagreed another student, "this image of the friend and the sword and the blood is arbitrary. You might as well be thinking of a snail. It's just something to distract you from the passion at hand."

"It's not arbitrary at all," said a third student. "Reb Aryeh said it's a friend lying dead on the battlefield. A friend is someone you love and so imagining harm to him is reminding you of the importance of love in the world. Love is more important than anger or lust. Love surely can't be a passion that comes from the Serpent, can it be?"

"There is no human love without divine love," the rabbi said. "The love between friends depends on the love of God. As for why the image of a friend wounded grotesquely on the battlefield distracts you from base passion, or a son slain before his time—most of you are too young even to guess at the consequences of anger. As it is written, 'Anger rests in the bosom of fools.' Before it eats you like a worm from the inside, before it consumes your life, anger can cause you to do great harm to others—your enemies and also your friends. Can you imagine any connection between your friend lying dead on the battlefield and your own anger that makes the image more useful than that of a snail?"

"Your friend might die because of your own anger," said the third student. "You are fellow soldiers, closer than brothers, you love him and he loves you—a love, as Reb Aryeh says, that reflects your mutual love of the Lord. But if you're angry at him for just one moment, then you might take your eye off him just when another soldier approaches with his sword drawn and your friend needs you to defend him the most. If you're angry at him, then you might even, God forbid, wish him dead, and God might hear your words and allow it to happen. And then, as Reb Aryeh says, you too would feel as if you had died, or might take your own life."

"But with all respect, isn't this an overinterpretation of the line 'For anger kills the foolish man,' Reb Aryeh?" asked the second student.

"Why do you think it is, as you say, an overinterpretation?" Reb Aryeh asked.

"Because a man who is angry will not, God forbid, take his own life," said the second student. "Anger is a passion and passions are the sign of the living."

The other students turned toward Reb Aryeh, as they instinctively did when class discussion may have gone too far. Perhaps the books that lay before him were never opened because his face was open book enough; anything he felt could be read there. He rubbed his eyes, then pressed his palms against his closed lids. Who knows how long he stayed like this, for in the presence of this great man, no matter what he was doing, the students lost track of time. Reb Aryeh revealed his face and said, wearily, "You don't need me to tell you, at your age, that the force of passion is in us all. Your chief aim— our chief aim—is to transfer the force of passion from the Serpent unto holiness. I don't know if an angry man, God forbid, would be tempted to take his own life. But if he were so tempted, then he must cultivate the desire to do a mitzvah, he must turn his temptation for destruction into some creative act. And let us say your passion is for money. Then instead of buying more objects or a bigger house, spend it on holy things. Give it to the poor. Or if your money means you do not have to work so hard, then in your leisure do not loaf but pass it studying Torah. And if your love is for food, then eat with joy and with attachment to the Creator. And eat only healthy foods so that you might have the strength to pray to the Lord, to stand there before Him all day long as tall as a tree. A passion for drink? Well, the Lord has blessed you with a challenge to turn this one into holiness."

The students laughed, then sat there quietly. Finally Zev, whose presence in class had never been advertised by the sound of his voice, said, "It doesn't work."

Zev had left the nighttime interview with his father feeling somehow diminished. Overnight he gave up responsibility for his brother's soul. And he stopped going to the lake. There was no point. It made no difference whether he breathed faster and harder or slower and softer; he moved no closer to God. He had stopped looking at his brother at night but he thought about him even more.

And now, because of this outrageous show of disrespect toward his father, Zev's days and those of the children he would never have would be cut off from the earth. He flung out what little he had left to lose. "I've tried thinking of things," Zev said, "not exactly like a friend with a sword coming out of his neck but similar. I've tried thinking of many different things. The first thing that comes to your head doesn't help, because it's too much like the thing you're trying not to think about. The second thing doesn't help either. You have to have a certain thing, as the rabbi said, something you can think of that has nothing to do with what you're trying not to think about. If your mind always goes to this thing, it can help—but only a little. It doesn't help very much. It's very hard not to think about something, especially certain things. It's very hard."

Zev seemed to be close to tears, and now he looked around at his classmates imploringly, as if to ask, *Which one of you will have the courage to say that you have felt what I have felt? Who here will say that what the rabbi is telling us to do doesn't work?*

But the other students were looking at their teacher. He always knew when to speak and when to remain silent. Now, with his gaze directed toward the table, he seemed absent. His hands came together but continued to move, twisting in opposite directions, as of their own will.

Profiting from this standstill, Zev went on. "Reb Aryeh, about the passion for money you say to turn it into a mitzvah by studying. Also the passion for food—you don't say to stop eating, you say to strengthen yourself to pray. And what about anger? Must we never be angry, or can anger too be turned to good?"

"Absolutely," said Reb Aryeh. The other students were amazed that this freak, this shameful creature that their teacher himself had created, would be the one to return the rabbi's spirit to his body. "Anger at a student—if we should take but one example—is warranted if the goal is to save the student's soul. If a teacher's anger at a student causes him to change his ways, then his anger has been turned to good."

"And what of the anger of a student toward his teacher?" Zev asked.

VII

From the moment his brother made his heretical confession, Zev wondered—he let himself wonder—what it must be like to live in a world without God. It was, he decided, like this, the marketplace, which he was making his way through now. There was no straight path through it. You couldn't run if you wanted to, you had to make your way around a sea of wagons. You had to watch your step. Horses, cows, people from as far away as the district center—people who didn't know who Zev was scattered among all those who only pretended they didn't. Smell of shit and fish and smoke, terrified squawking of birds, babble of voices, deceitful smiles, hands extended, money taken. Partitions, stalls, tables, overhangs—all of it temporary, all of it illusion. The only things permanent in the square were the black obelisk, crowned on two sides with three crosses rising along a single shaft, and the cobblestones themselves, which were crowded now with cooking pots and piles of cloth and baskets of vegetables and barrels of grains. If there was order here, it couldn't be discerned. The market was held only once a week, but no weeds dared grow between the cobblestones or where they were missing.

Zev's mother vended a putty made of boiled rye flour and chalk and oil. It was used by the town's carpenters and painters, and it had such a reputation for strength that merchants from the district center came to trade for it as well. Isaac with his powerful arms put up and took down her stall and served as her assistant. The stalls were on the far side of the square and Zev tried to avoid them, but he was being pushed in that direction by the crowd. His mother called out his name, too loud, the single syllable like a knife thrust through the rough fabric of the marketplace. Everyone who had pretended to ignore him turned and stared, and as he approached he saw on his mother's face a certain satisfaction scratching through her usual defiance.

"What are you doing here?" she asked, wiping her forehead with her apron.

"I came to see Isaac."

And where was her so-called assistant?

"He's gone to let my usual customers know I'm here." But where else would she be on this day? Here was a world in which lies were apparently allowed. "You should be in school," she said with a knowing gaze.

He looked down, as his father taught. To be among those who are humbled but do not humble others; are scorned but do not reply. Even here in the marketplace he could not abide by its rules, or its freedom from them. *I have come to bring Isaac a message,* he wanted to say. *I have come to bring a message from Reb Aryeh. I have come to feel what I have so long wanted to feel.*

He would have liked to say all three things to his mother and let her try to distinguish lies from truth.

He left her but didn't head back in the direction of his father's school. He pushed his way instead toward the far side of the square, where the road to the district center began. Zev had never been to the district center. The lake, which was not so far away, was as far as he had ever dared escape. He would be imprisoned in the town forever, just as he was already imprisoned in his own useless body. At least he knew this. He didn't stupidly believe, as his stupid brother did, that he would make it to America, where you ate meat every day and there was work for everyone and all the women were beautiful.

Across the square Isaac was smiling his easy smile as he spoke with two other boys, neither of them Jewish. One of the boys was colorless, obviously a follower. The other was Josef.

Zev's blood galloped in his ears. He had the impression that his heart wasn't beating more quickly than usual, but that the cavity in which it hung was otherwise hollow. And if this emptiness wasn't an absence of fear, then it could at least allow courage to rush in. By now Josef had noticed him, and Zev saw he had no trace of fear in his eyes, as everyone else in the town did when Zev approached. No trace even of surprise, though the market was not Zev's world and he rarely came here. Zev held Josef's gaze too. He was not handsome, this Josef, but his wide face contributed to the impression of solidity that his broad-shouldered body gave. Both Isaac and the other boy were laughing—but Zev couldn't imagine Josef ever laughing. And then Isaac noticed Josef staring, and he followed the line of his gaze to Zev.

"It's the little rabbi," the third boy hastily put in, to make up for being the last to notice him.

"Go home," Isaac said.

But Zev just stood there.

Now the third boy, the dull one, was really interested. "Why don't you go to the synagogue," he sneered.

"Zev!" Isaac said.

"Go blow the horn in the synagogue," the third one said and moved to block him from escaping.

Zev could smell liquor on his breath. If the boy was afraid to be in Zev's presence, he wasn't showing it, except perhaps in the slight tremble of his legs as he stood there before him. Clearly, this one wanted to hurt Zev in order to raise himself in Josef's esteem. Josef, who in his brother's stories never needed to take more than one step to dissolve the opposing front line of would-be boy soldiers. Josef, who wielded his power by withholding, by never giving his opponents what they so desperately wanted.

When Zev stepped out of his shadow, more to make something happen than to escape, the third boy stayed where he was. They were letting Zev go—a clear path to safety lay before him. And so Isaac never had to defend him, though Zev was no longer sure he would.

The lake at summer's end. Nothing was as Zev remembered. The lake, the trees, the clearing where he had sat—all of it had changed in the usual way, the way the world was always changing. It was not so very late in the day but the water was colorless, the sun having already fallen behind the tops of the trees. A carpet of dead leaves crunched under his shoes. But it was still hot. The light was thick and heavy and still. It seemed to have poured from heaven before the sun had gone. Filtered its way through the branches and stopped, stiffened there like amber or glue. For this was the real change, not the plants that had withered in the drought or the leaves that had fallen but the impression the scene gave of stillness, trees and water and grass having fused into one, all of it held together by the solid mass of light. A paradox: flow and stasis, the world a record of its own creation.

Tomorrow he would be fifteen, a number that happened to be the value of nothing more than one of the names of God. A number that blessedly had nothing to do with fires. Fifteen meant only this, that another year had passed during which he had failed to master the passions of his body.

He lowered his pants and saw how his jacket and shirt and fringed underclothes hung down and continued to cover him. His clothes made his body into something unrecognizable as a body. Turned him into a scholar, no longer a man—the way a woman in her wedding gown is no longer a woman but a bride, the way a person wrapped in a funeral shroud is a corpse. He took off everything he was wearing—even his hat. He laid them down on the leaves, placed them next to each other as on himself, so that a flattened man seemed to lie there.

Pale as a grub, he stood under his meditation tree and breathed in and out. Then he headed toward the lake, walking with calm to its pebbled edge.

He put one toe in. Took a step. He was walking on rocks, dark now around the paleness of his foot, which was fully submerged. He took another step and the water lapped at his ankles. Left foot, then right, then left again, then right—he tried not to count the steps. The water was not cold. But as he walked he braced himself for the drop-off into the freezing netherworld. He closed his eyes and said the *sh'ma*, as he had been taught to say before death.

He did not see the Divine Throne. He did not see the beautiful woman. He saw his father sitting in the schoolroom with the holy texts spread open. Writing the book that Zev now understood was for him.

He stopped moving and turned around. The shore lay at some distance but his knees were not wet. The water was warm against his naked legs.

Acknowledgments

I live and write in a household of three, but it took a shtetl to bring this book to fruition.

My parents filled me with stories and learning—and let me use their beach cottage to work.

My old friend Susan Buchsbaum was my sounding board and a careful reader of the stories in this book.

Anne Cheng has given me deep friendship and excellent feedback on my work.

Cappy Coates and Veronica Selver provided indispensable comments and edits, as well as encouragement over the years.

Tim Dean deserves much credit for slogging through my early writing.

Simon Firth read my work over the years and helped me with "There's Hope for Us All."

Kirby Gann and Sarah Gorham fearlessly and tastefully line-edited this book, teaching me a lot about storytelling in the process.

Dylan Glockler has used his formidable technical and visual skills to make me multimedia.

David King honored me with his beautiful cover art.

Sala Levin and Nadine Epstein edited "Blue" and gave me a break and a forum to be read.

Jay Michaelson brought his vast and varied wisdom to the title story and its world.

Tim Pauly was an early reader of most of the stories in this book and showed great forbearance during our photo shoot.

Chris Riscinitti taught me about martial arts as he pumped me up.

Mark Rhynsburger was a skillful proofreader and an insightful reader of these stories.

Salvatore Scibona has my gratitude for choosing my book and showing such interest in me as a writer. His example inspires me to keep on.

Kristina Youso helped me imagine the world of the museum more fully.

Tim Pauly / www.fototim.net

JASON K. FRIEDMAN was born in Savannah, Georgia, and earned a BA from Yale and an MA from the Johns Hopkins Writing Seminars. His work has appeared in literary journals and anthologies including *Best American Gay Fiction* and the cultural-studies reader *Goth: Undead Subculture*. He has published two children's books, including the thriller *Phantom Trucker*. He was the runner-up in the Associated Writing Programs Award Series in the Novel, and he won the *Moment Magazine*–Karma Foundation Short Fiction Contest for "Blue," the opening story in *Fire Year*. Jason works as a technical writer in San Francisco, where he lives with his husband, filmmaker Jeffrey Friedman, and their dog, Lefty.

Sarabande Books thanks you for the purchase of this book; we do hope you enjoy it! Founded in 1994 as an independent, nonprofit, literary press, Sarabande publishes poetry, short fiction, and literary nonfiction—genres increasingly neglected by commercial publishers. We are committed to producing beautiful, lasting editions that honor exceptional writing, and to keeping those books in print. If you're interested in further reading, take a moment to browse our website, www.sarabandebooks.org. There you'll find information about other titles; opportunities to contribute to the Sarabande mission; and an abundance of supporting materials including audio, video, a lively blog, and our Sarabande in Education program.